Sarah M. H. Gardner

Quaker Idyls

Sarah M. H. Gardner

Quaker Idyls

ISBN/EAN: 9783337398583

Printed in Europe, USA, Canada, Australia, Japan

Cover: Foto ©Andreas Hilbeck / pixelio.de

More available books at **www.hansebooks.com**

QUAKER IDYLS

BY

SARAH M. H. GARDNER

NEW YORK

HENRY HOLT AND COMPANY

1894

CONTENTS.

*This little book is
affectionately dedicated to two
dear " Friends,"*

E. W. P. and M. M. T.

TWELFTH STREET
MEETING.

QUAKER IDYLS.

TWELFTH STREET
MEETING.

ARE the summer mornings longer in Philadelphia than elsewhere, or is it the admirable Quaker custom of breaking the fast at the usual hour on Sunday that gives such delightful leisure before the calm walk to meeting at half past ten ?

Certain it is that the Sabbath of June 11 was no exception to the general rule, and when John and Martha Wilson, with their daughter Cassy, passed beyond

the brick wall which separates the
sanctuary from the street, there
were groups of Friends kindly inquiring after the welfare of each
other, and offering greeting to
such as were unaccustomed to the
place.

John passed to the right, where
he extended his hand to a fellow-
worshiper. Martha paused in the
doorway to stroke the shining
curls of a pretty child, whose gentle mother had failed in her efforts
to subdue Dame Nature. And
Cassy, sweet Cassy, who was no
longer very young, felt the color
rise, and modestly dropped her
eyes, as she noticed the pleased
observance of her entrance de-
picted on the face of George
Evans, already occupying a seat
on the "men's side" of the meeting-house.

Several elderly Friends were in

their place on the floor, and in the
gallery were those who held the
positions of elders and accepted
ministers. Their hands were
folded, and one or two of the men,
who held walking sticks, rested
their hands on the rounded tops.
But the faces of all wore a far-
away look, as if the present surroundings could never disturb the
sweet serenity of their souls.

Quietly the congregation gathered. There was not a large company. But few wore the garb of
the past generation. There was,
among the middle-aged, a disposition to grow a little plainer with
increasing years, but the soft felt
hat was conspicuous in the room,
and the stiff bonnets were relieved by silk shirrs of brown or
gray.

Cassy, this warm day, has assumed a gown of white stuff, the

very essence of simplicity ; a straw bonnet of half modern date, destitute of embellishment, unless the satin ties, reaching halfway to the crown, and the blond pleating surrounding her face, could be called trimming. The dress was closed at the throat by a small gold clasp, which confined also the edges of the linen collar ; drab, openwork mitts covered her well-shaped hands—hands that were never weary with good work, nor ever fearful of losing their beauty in the performance of the daily toils that fell upon them.

As the house grew silent, and more silent, a gentle prayer went up from her heart that she might keep her spirit undefiled, and when, after a little, the stillness was broken by the voice of an aged man in the upper seat, she raised her head and paid the strictest attention to his opening words.

" Like as a father pitieth his children," he began, his pale face reflecting the purity of his aspirations, and the trembling voice, growing in volume as he proceeded, until after a few moments it had fallen into that peculiar cadence, a sort of half melancholy rising and falling inflection, measured and monotonous, that afflicts the unaccustomed ear, and so often in these holy assemblies destroys their solemnity.

Philo Thomas was a trial to poor Cassy ; she revered his patient life of tribulation, she caught the reflection of the light which glowed within his soul, but his outward manifestations were singularly unacceptable to her ; she wished that so good a man might feel called upon to keep silence in public places, and yet she half rebuked herself for the seeming disrespect.

Patiently she tried to keep pace with the thought that so slowly fell from the sing-song utterance, but gradually she drifted into a different channel. The glowing face of the man who had rejoiced at her coming was rising before her. Educated, as she had been, to the strictest truthfulness, she could not even seek to shut out from herself the knowledge that she felt and enjoyed his satisfaction at her presence there, nor, indeed, her own pleasure and comfort in this state of affairs. Her heart beat a trifle faster than it ought, and the blush burned again as she forgot the preacher and the company and only remembered the one face across the narrow line which divided the women from the men.

Suddenly the voice ceased, and the solemn silence smote her like a sword.

"What have I done!" she cried out in spirit, "I have desecrated the holy place. My thoughts are the thoughts of a worldling! Can I bear through the week the recollection that I wasted my opportunity on the first day? that any human being can have the power to turn me from my path, can destroy my self-respect, can make me forget my Creator?"

"The Lord is in his holy temple, blessed be the name of the Lord," passed through her heart, and formed on her trembling lips. Hot tears filled her eyes and fell unheeded on her handkerchief, tears of shame and humiliation.

A faint rustle aroused her. In

the gallery a slight pale woman arose, untied the strings of her stiff bonnet, and laid it on the bench beside her. Stepping forward until her hand rested on the rail in front, she spoke softly, distinctly, and the happy change from the droning tones of the earlier speaker riveted the attention of the wandering.

She spoke of the pure in heart; defining her terms, dwelling on the growth of sin if permitted to linger, emphasizing the truth that we must be ever on the alert to discern the shadow of transgression, until poor Cassy—who had at once entered into the spirit of the sermon—poor Cassy felt that this was being spoken directly to her.

Then as the sweet voice paused, a new measure filled it. She turned from admonition to ador-

ation, depicting the joy there is
in heaven over one sinner who
returns from his ways, and as
if carrying out the thought of
the aged man who had preceded
her, and which he had so sorely
missed in his illustration, she
urged the tenderness of an earthly
parent to an erring child, and the
abounding love and beneficence
of our Heavenly Father.

"Dear children," she cried,
"do not fear to approach him.
Open your hearts! Search out
the hidden places! Let the light
stream in and your sins shall be
wiped away. Fear not man ; that
which it is impressed upon you
to reveal, dare not to keep
secret."

She resumed her seat and her
bonnet, but the seed she had
sown took deep root in Cassy's
heart. All through the remaining

hour she revolved its teaching in her soul. It was clear the meaning for her was a stronger and heartier purification of her thoughts. Not that George Evans was an unholy object, nor that his affection was to be despised, but that the meeting-house was not the place for human admiration. And oh! what did these words mean, "Not to keep silent?" Was she bidden to unfold this page to George, to tell him that the lesson was for him also?

What pain it cost her to dream of such a task! yet was not this one of those hidden places that should be flooded with light? What if he did deem *her* unwomanly who could speak on such a matter without having been spoken to? Were not the commands of the Lord to be preferred to any earthly comfort? She should perhaps lose her lover—see herself dethroned, for. never a word had he vouchsafed her but of the plainest courtesy, but she should gain the respect of her own conscience. The fires that purify, also blister and burn. How could she refuse? Perhaps George Evans' soul was in peril too, for well she knew that upon his ear had fallen unheeded the words of the first preacher.

Solemnly the two men friends at the head of the gallery clasped hands, and immediately a little hum of neighborly inquiry went round.

Cassy dreaded to move. She felt, rather than saw, her lover waiting for her outside the door, and silently asking help in her time of trouble, she walked down the aisle. She did not omit any of the customary greetings; she promised to meet with the sewing committee the next day, to carry jelly to an aged friend, and turned and shook the hand which George Evans held out to her.

There was nothing strange that he walked beside her down Arch Street, but he gave her little opportunity to open her heart. They had passed but a short distance when he broke the silence by saying :

"Cassy, does thee know I almost felt that Mary Elwood's sermon was intended for me ? And perhaps for thee, too. I have thought for some time that the Lord had designed thy path and mine to run side by side. Thee knows that this morning was the first opportunity I have had to attend meeting for several weeks, but when I saw thy face it was so pleasant to me that I fell into a worldly train of thought—how I might tell thee of my great hope, that thee would respond to my affection for thee. Mary Elwood's voice broke my reverie, and showed me where my way led. I resolved then to speak to thee at once, for something in thy look betrayed thy feeling, and I feared I had led thee into evil ; that my glance, as I entered meeting, had possessed the power of withdrawing thy meditation from the Lord, and the voice of his servant warned me to repent, and hesitate not to reveal to thee the source of my inquietude."

Gravely she laid her hand upon his arm, and with but one shy upward glance at his earnest face, she said solemnly :

"Blessed be the name of the Lord. This lesson was also revealed unto me. Had thee not felt called upon to warn me against such temptation, I should have dwelt upon it to thee at the first opportunity, but our Heavenly Father hath spared me the trial."

A QUAKER WEDDING.

A QUAKER WEDDING.

RENOWNED foreigner characterized Philadelphia as a " city of magnificent sameness." Possibly this is true of the older portions of the town, and surely there is little in the exterior of the compactly built houses on upper Arch Street to distinguish the dwelling of the Twelfth Street Friend from that of a more worldly citizen.

On a certain morning in October, the same atmosphere of seclusion surrounded the whole block between Sixteenth and Seventeenth streets. No possible hint came forth from No. — that within its red brick walls, outlined with

the cold precision of white marble
sills and doorsteps and guarded
by heavy shutters, there was about
to be consummated a tender little
drama.   The narrow door, with its
painted icy glare and glistening
knob, opened at short intervals to
admit tall figures in long coats,
cut with straight collars, and bea-
ver hats in gray or black, whose
broad brims shadowed smooth-
shaven, manly faces.   Trim little
maidens too, and their quaint
feminine relatives, waited demurely on the spotless step, for
the opening touch of a dark-
skinned hand within.

It rarely happened that a newcomer entered without a pleasant
greeting to the elderly colored
woman: "How is thee to-day,
Hannah?" or, "I am glad to find
thee has conquered thy rheuma-
tism"; which brought a low-voiced

answer : " Thank thee ; will thee
go up to the second story, or can
I send thy bonnet ? " This to
the elder women, while the sweet
young damsels, in a happy sub-
dued flutter, have turned to the
guest chamber to smooth their
silken raiment, or possibly to ven-
ture so far toward personal adorn-
ment as the fastening of a few
white buds over the dainty cor-
sage. There was a little murmur
of soft voices : the expression of
joy that Cassy and George had
been blessed with such a beautiful
wedding day; the hope that
Mary Anna Landers would be able
to reach there in time for the
ceremony. " She always speaks
so acceptably to the young."
One told of a certain aged Friend
in deep affliction and the message
that she bore from the dying bed
to the gentle bride whose helpful

hands had so often soothed the
pain away. And thus, in groups,
the guests descended to the parlor, the straight long room where
a strong light from tall windows
in front and rear was modified by
means of drab Venetian blinds.
Between these windows hung, on
one hand, a modest engraving of
William Penn, and upon the opposite wall that of Elizabeth Fry.
Both were framed in dark-colored
wood, and the benign expression
of the gifted man, and the wealth
of dignity in the face of the cele-
brated philanthropist charmed in
spite of their austere surroundings. Upon a marble mantel,
under a glass shade, rested a
clock, as white and cold as the
slab beneath ; a small basket of
delicate ferns, as if half ashamed
of their vivid green, retired behind the solemn mouth of a tall

undecorated silver candlestick. The room was well-nigh filled with chairs placed in regular order, and two hair-cloth sofas whose broad seats accommodated the elders of the meeting. Directly below the picture of the venerable Penn were the places designed for George and Cassy, straight-backed old oaken chairs, that would be a delight to the antiquarian of to-day, and near the right wall stood a small table upon which rested a roll of parchment, a pen, and a substantial ink-well.

One of the windows was open, and the fresh sweet air came in laden with the noises of the street : the rumble of the carts, the click of hoofs upon the sharp stone pavements, the distant cries of venders, and the whistle of the locomotive. The light breeze stirred the cap borders and the kerchiefs of the placid women, who lifted their soft hands to re-arrange the muslin with the same instinct that prompts the care of curl and ornament in their fashion-able sisters. The parchment flut-tered to the ground, and in re-placing it there was exposed to view a page of exquisite penman-ship, the great letters in ornate Old English hardly belonging to Quaker simplicity.

Meanwhile in the sitting room at the head of the first flight of stairs there was a sweet picture. This apartment was so entirely an ema-nation from the home life that the stiffness and coldness of the lower room was totally lacking. The very loud tick of the old-fashioned mahogany clock that stood in the corner had a sound of cheer. The little wood fire on the hearth gave out a welcome, and the half dozen rockers and lounging chairs in gray and brown dress held open arms. A big Maltese cat crouched by the rug, a few pencil sketches from the hand of a favorite nephew graced the wall, and a heavy bookcase gave evidence thro' its glass door, of much substantial learning. There was a cluster of periodicals on a stand, the clear title of " The Friend " recalling their import ; a stereoscope with a tray of views, a basket of knitting work, and, hanging on the back of a peculiar easy-chair, the round pillow that betokens snatches of rest.

Cassy was standing by the east window. The broad beams of the morning sun were growing more direct, and fell with force over her delicate form. Her gown of silver gray enveloped her like

mist, and chastened the rising
color. As she turned toward
the advancing figure of the
bridegroom, her eyes suffused
with tears. She held forth her
hands and said tremblingly, " Dear
George, how earnestly I pray that
our Heavenly Father may ever
guide me so that I walk aright,
and fulfill toward thee all the re-
quirements of this holy relation."
Tenderly he kissed her as he replied, " My soul is assured that
thee never would have been drawn
so close to me were it not the
will of the Divine Master : " and
presently when John and Martha
entered they pressed the daughter
to their hearts and breathed upon
the stalwart young man a blessing, so full of emotion that the
patience of awaiting Friends was
quite forgotten. Then the tall
monitor on the corner, that had

marked the hour of Cassy's birth, gave warning of another epoch in her life.

The company was seated as the little party entered the parlor. George and Cassy advanced to the chairs assigned them, John and Martha next their daughter, and the parents of George occupied a similar position on the other side. There were a few minutes of absolute silence, then the younger pair arose, joined hands, and in a clear unbroken voice the bridegroom spoke these words :

"In the presence of the Lord and this assembly, I, George Evans take Cassy Wilson to be my wife, promising with Divine assistance to be unto her a faithful and loving husband until death shall separate us ; " and after an instant's pause, the bride, with a far-away look in her sweet eyes, calmly repeated the same tender promise. Then they sat down again, and presently a white-haired man, with so great revelation of power in his face that it might almost have been called conscious strength, appeared in supplication before the throne of grace. He asked that the twain now made one might become nearer and dearer to each other as time went on, and that in fulfillment of the claims of the spirit, they might ever be ready to respond to the call of the Bridegroom who cometh while it is yet night. For some moments after the prayer had ended the company remained with bowed heads, and the stillness was but gently broken by the movement of another honored Friend, who came forward as a member of the committee appointed by the monthly meeting, to be present at the marriage and report that all proceedings had taken place in strict accordance with the rules of the society. He now read aloud the certificate, heretofore lying on the table, testifying to such regularity, and advancing to the bridal pair requested them to affix their signatures. The pen was then passed to the parents, and as each person present gave hands to the happy, George and Cassy, the same favor was extended. During the conclusion of this ceremony, Cassy's color had brightened with the congratulations and gentle admonitions of these so dear to her, and before it was finished the little buzz of friendly interest had wreathed the placid face in smiles, and dried the tears that were almost too ready to start to the eyes of the tender mother. No one was forgotten ; even the faithful Hannah and the Cassius of long service added their irregular strokes to the certificate, and Cassy caught up on her arm the three-year-old guest, and guided his playful fingers over the smooth page.

There was a quiet intimation that a collation was spread in an adjoining apartment, and the thrifty folk, who scorn the embellishments but not the substantials of life, did ample justice to the bounteous repast, daintily served from the finest of linen, the clearest of glasses, and the frailest of china. There was no spoken word of thanksgiving, only a pause wherein their hearts might acknowledge the mercies of the Giver of all Good. There was no haste, no indecorous indulgence in the temptations of the table, but a cheerful, happy tone pervaded the company who regarded marriage not as the absorption of one life by another, but as a true union of strong souls for the furtherance of God's holy purpose.

As each guest departed, he or she was freighted with a package of wedding cake for some friend or servant: "Maria, will thee kindly give this to Eldridge Percy? We all feel to regret his absence, and trust that he may be spared to meet with us once again." "Philip, thee knows how dear our Cassy was to Hagar the summer we spent at your home; thee will not mind carrying her a bit of cake?"

And when at length the hour of parting came, there was no long line of merrymakers to hurl slippers and showers of rice after the retreating carriage, but there were last words spoken that dwelt in the hearts of the earnest young husband and wife, and the injunction of the father was a simple admonition to " search ever for the light that is revealed in the soul"; and the loving children heard his brave voice reply to the neighbor that regretted the distance that must henceforth seprate them : " I can safely trust my son and daughter in the hands of the Lord, wheresoever he may lead them."

TWO GENTLEWOMEN.

TWO GENTLEWOMEN.

HE square brick house with many windows, in the little village of W., was called the "Mountain Place," both from the name of one of its occupants, and also from its situation, which was the most conspicuous point in town.

The owner was a rich manufacturer, who had for many years placed it at the disposal of his two widowed sisters less prosperous, financially, than himself.

Mrs. Letitia Mountain's family lived on the lower floor in a commodious suite of "apartments," hardly known as such in that day, when any respectable person was supposed to occupy, or furnish, an entire dwelling, but the idiosyncracy was in this case excused on ground of a peculiar attachment existing between the sisters.

The double parlors, with high ceiling and heavy folding doors, were forever resplendent in white china paint and velvet paper, and the visitor felt almost obliged to observe the extreme complexity of the figure on the carpet, evidently designed for homes of heroic proportions.

The upper rooms were far less imposing, and thus better·suited to the smaller purse and household of the elder sister, Mrs. Honora Plum. This poor lady endured much from the companionship of a stepdaughter, ill-tempered and idle, and reflecting the blaze of an ancient es-

cutcheon stained by vice, for Mrs.
Plum had married the younger
son of a titled English gentleman.

Nothing of the regret from
which she must have suffered
ever passed her lips, and her patient smile sweetened the loaf
which she so generously shared
with the woman whose only claim
was the name she bore.

Mrs. Mountain's past, on the
contrary, was delightful to con-
template. A happy marriage in
early life shed a halo over even
the long illness and death of a beloved husband ; but neither this
break in the tide of joy, nor the
sorrows of Honora, ever darkened
the light of true sister love that
doubled their present portion of
helpfulness and cheer.

Both ladies were short and dark,
with large brown eyes which never
lost their sparkle, and well-formed

lips that kept a rosy color into late years.

Fashion forever stamps some part of Nature's work as reprehensible, and at the period of which I write, the gray locks that represent intensity of feeling as often as age were considered unfit to be seen by the world. So the heavy silken bands that graced the brows of both sisters were closely covered with beribboned caps, and bordered with "false fronts" of dusky hair, coiled on each side over two small combs, forming stiff and ungainly puffs that did not seem to belong to the little women, but to which they were so much attached that one never admitted the other to her chamber until the structure was erected, or a huge nightcap entirely concealed the absence of it.

Far more suitable would have

been the simplicity of the Friend's costume, which bore a wondrous charm for them, as the dress of their beloved mother. But the sisters had wandered from the fold, each had married "out of meeting" and thereby forfeited her birthright membership; and having renounced the worship of their fathers, they also felt it incumbent to robe themselves somewhat according to the fashion of the world's people, but the "Stranger" air which marked their devotions before a "hireling ministry" also clung to their garments.

It was a little pitiful, this estrangement from their early religious associations, and perchance it might have been their greatest pleasure to return to the fold when the days of their widowhood came, but the meeting was held in a remote district of the township, and neither of the sisters was robust. For this reason they made a church home in the nearest house of worship, and carried thither so much of their elementary religion as wrought daily miracles of love and patience.

They were charitable to a degree almost beyond praise, and the fine bearing, the impressive presence of the little pair, could have come from nothing else than a realization of noble attributes.

The annals of New York indeed would be incomplete without mention of the exceeding service rendered the State in time of need by a rich Quaker, who steadfastly refused any public recognition, but whose death was everywhere heralded as that of a man combining in his character modesty and rare worth.

Perhaps it was the conscious-

ness of being heir to these virtues
that led Honora into a false con-
ception of the inheritance of her
husband, but the painful knowledge of her error never lessened
her understanding of the motto
" Noblesse oblige."

Everybody forgave the sisters
their touch of pride since both its
source and outcome were of such
purity, but it was almost pathetic
to hear their personal disavowal
of merit, attributing all things of
worth in their admirable woman-
hood to their ancestry, and when,
in the days of her children's youth,
Mrs. Mountain found it necessary
to chastise them, the rod was considered far less severe than a reminder that through misdemeanor
they were sullying the family
record.

It was a matter of deep regret
to both Honora and Letitia that

they had no sons. The former was childless, and the latter had buried her boys in infancy, but it was a consolation that the marriage of their brother, late in life, had resulted in securing a continuance of the honored line.

Hospitality was one of the inherited virtues. The fruit cake jar was never allowed to become empty, and on such holidays as were not bespoken by their brother, their separate tables were surrounded by the impecunious old and young of their acquaintance.

So long as Mrs. Mountain's daughters remained unmarried there was an abundance of merry-making, but after they had gone to homes of their own this youthful element was greatly missed. Mrs. Plum's stepdaughter was too grim to be social, and gradually the lives of the sisters fell into a routine.

Certain days in the month were devoted to family visits. The rector was entertained by them alternately, at stated periods, and once every fortnight they dressed themselves in stiff silks and real laces, and went through the formality of returning calls. No doubt the conversation was as little varied as the wardrobe, yet it was a pleasing duty, faithfully performed.

They had been educated like the majority of well-to-do women of that period, but this was far from developing a love of study— that progressive intelligence which furnishes the ladies of the present with unfailing entertainment.

Nothing, therefore, was a greater satisfaction to them than the daily visits of an old and respected colonel, living on a large farm just beyond the border of the town.

He rode to the post office every morning on a white horse, quite as stiff in his joints as his master, and it was one of the duties of the postman to respond to the timely cough of the colonel by carrying out the scanty mail, if such there chanced to be. The soldierly salutation repaid him a hundred-fold for this small attention, while the colonel turned his horse toward Mountain Place.

He was so prompt in all his proceedings that the servant prepared herself, at ten o'clock, to answer the summons of the enormous brass knocker, and with as much dignity as if he had come with a message of state, the ruddy man inquired for " the ladies." Then, as he entered the hall, he graciously relieved any embarrass-

ment by mentioning " Mrs. Mountain's parlor, if you please," or
" Mrs. Plum's drawing room,"
alternating day by day. Immediately the lady presiding arose and
greeted him as though he was recently returned from a foreign
mission, and in the next breath
spoke to the servant, who had
long ago learned to await this
direction : " Ask Mrs. Plum if it
will be convenient to come down,
Colonel Gray is here," or " My
compliments to Mrs. Mountain."

The newcomer then formally
welcomed the second sister, carefully asked after her health, and
conversation became general.

An hour, sometimes two, the
colonel's horse stood in the wind
and weather awaiting his agree-
able master, but if, as rarely happened, the latter limit was trans-
gressed, a loud neighing brought

the gentleman to his feet. " Ladies, I have had a most entertaining morning ; duty alone calls me from your side. Allow me to wish you good-day."

In the afternoon as the sisters sat by the front window knitting socks for the poor, or daintily stitching some fine muslin for a baby's outfit, they discussed the Colonel's visit.

" Letitia, I am sorry brother does not like the Colonel."

They never disagreed, and from a constant desire to emphasize, each the opinion of the other, there had grown a habit of repetition.

" Yes, Honora, I wish brother did incline toward the Colonel."

" I cannot understand his objection. Colonel Grey is a gentleman, and an excellent provider."

This term embraced a multitude

of small virtues, chiefly that of generosity toward his immediate family, and to Mrs. Mountain and Mrs. Plum, the man who failed in this respect had better not be alluded to.

It was a little strange that they knew the Colonel's household habits, for he lived alone with an aged housekeeper and her husband, and it was only at long intervals that he opened his doors to his friends, albeit he was justly proud of the frequent honor he enjoyed of "drinking a dish of tea" at the Mountain Place, and on these occasions he never forgot to be strictly impartial in his attentions, and addressed his conversation first to one, then to the other of the sisters.

Like the entire village population, he was well aware that to these ladies everyone looked for advice, and indeed for intelligent nursing. So frequent were the midnight calls for services that one of the servant's regular duties was the disposition at nightfall of their hoods, cloaks, and lantern conveniently near the front door.

A reference to this formed a staple joke between the friends, and Letitia frequently asserted (and it was repeated by Honora) that in case of illness at " Moss Farm," they would consider themselves engaged.

Perhaps the good Colonel had more than a jest at heart when he referred to the matter, for the ills of life come surely in train of age, and the summons reached Mountain Place on an early morning of September. It was a shock to the ladies, this forerunner of a parting from one who had been so stanch a friend, and so inconsiderate a visitor, as their brother insisted.

Just as the carryall came in sight of the Colonel's homestead, the first twitter of awakening birds brought a new sense of life and activity into the world. The dark forest behind the house sent forth a thousand notes of welcome to the day, and the clear spring, where the old horse turned to drink, added its gentle murmur.

Mrs. Mountain was touched, her eyes moistened.

"Alas!" she said, noting the movement of the old gray, "the world never stops for any of us. The birds sing, the horse wants to drink, the sunlight flashes over the farm, just as if the good man that has lived so long to lighten the cares of others, was not passing away."

"Passing away! Yes, passing

away," and the solemn voice of her sister, seemed like an echo from the hills.

It was the usual trouble, a shock of paralysis, and the faithful doctor gave little encouragement, yet he thought it possible the Colonel's speech might become clear again, and when the stupor that enthralled the poor man had passed, the pale eye wandered about the room. Words were unnecessary, the watchers understood that he wanted a hand laid in his own, and Letitia gently slid her soft palm beneath the chilled fingers. Honora as promptly took her place at the other side, stroking the withered arm that lay motionless upon the bed.

The doctor opened the window, and as the delicious breath of the pines crept in, the sick man stirred. He moved his head restlessly. But when Mrs. Mountain would have left her place to re-arrange his pillows, suddenly his tongue loosed and he spoke, fee-bly indeed, and with an effort, but the words fell distinctly upon the listeners.

"Years ago, I wanted—I in-tended she should be my wife if——" He stopped. Presently he gave evidence that the same thought was still in his mind.

"Yes," he murmured, "but I love her just as well."

The doctor moistened the dry lips, and the sisters both moved as if to assist, but one lifeless hand pressed heavily, and the poor member with a little vitality motioned Mrs. Mountain not to stir.

So they remained, while hour after hour went by.

The noonday was upon them

when again the old face brightened and the quavering voice said slowly :

"Yes, yes, I love her just as well."

The silence that followed was not broken again, and soon the faithful sisters spread the white sheet over the dear dead.

That night, as they sat together in Mrs. Mountain's stately parlor, Honora said with a sigh :

"Perhaps, Letitia, it is just as well the Colonel never spoke to you about marriage. His family was not so good as our own, but I thought it strange he could see you so often and not love you."

And Letitia startled Mrs. Plum by contradicting her.

"Child alive, Honora ! I always knew the Colonel loved the ground you trod on."

OUR LITTLE NEIGHBORS.

OUR LITTLE NEIGHBORS.

A first of April story.

ERRY came in one spring morning wearing a very triumphant air. He caught the baby from the floor and tossed him as he said :

" Well, Kittie, I have taken the house."

" Have you, dear? · Now do just tell me all about it. Is it ' The Cottage by the Sea' or a 'cobble-stone front' at Riverdale ? Have you plenty of neighbors, and a garden spot, and what rent? Pray don't keep me in suspense ! "

An amused smile passed over his face as he seated himself.

"Let me see, question No. 1. Is it the 'Cottage by the Sea?' Yes, if you choose, for the ocean is only three miles away; just a lovely drive or even walk through delicious pine wood. A 'cobble-stone front?' No, thank you. A small plain wooden box, of a dull gray color, well suited to its neighbors, for there is quite a community of Quakers in the vicinity. Neighbors near? Yes, decidedly, as our share is only half the box, after all. It was built for a summer home for two brothers, the Allens, next door to us, you know. Caleb cannot leave town this year, so we can occupy his quarters. Garden spot? Oh, yes; abundantly large, but all in one inclosure. The house is regularly divided, but the grounds are not. Don't look worried, little wife; you and I and the baby are

not likely to be troublesome, and
I am sure Joseph Allen's staid
household will behave itself."

And so on the " First of April"
we moved. My costume was con-
siderably demoralized when we
reached our summer home. The
baby had quite destroyed all the
beauty my hat ever had, and my
small nephew, who had insisted
upon going to visit us the first
day, was so timid in crossing the
river that he clung to my draperies
with too much fervor, and I pre-
sume that I was an object of pity
to the few ladies in the cabin.
Certain it is that I felt decidedly
shabby, tired, and perhaps a trifle
out of humor as I entered the cottage door and dropped my heavy
boy on the clean, but carpetless
floor. Bridget soon made her appearance with a list of the casual-
ties, and as Jerry had not yet ar-

rived, I was growing very gloomy when a light tap at the side entrance caused me to spring to my feet.

What a picture of simplicity and purity stood before me! I blushed at the contrast which my disordered finery presented! Here on my doorstep were two little wrens (I could call them nothing else, although they were certainly girls), one just a trifle taller and larger than the other; both with soft pink cheeks and brown hair cut close on the neck and parted smoothly and evenly, without a suggestion of crimp or curl. Their dresses were of a drab color, just visible below long white aprons, on which there was not even a superfluous button! Their linen sunbonnets boasted of no ruffles, and the colored stockings, which peeped from beneath

their rather long dresses, were of
the same shade. Little gray birds,
with just such shy little ways !

The elder one looked up timidly
and held toward me a basket, saying:

"Mother sent thee this lunch,"

"And don't forget, Sallie,"
whispered the younger, "don't
forget about the baby."

" Thee can ask that, Debby."

The only worldly looking fea-
ture between them was Debby's
blue eyes, and they sparkled and
ran riot in spite of her, but her
mouth was very serious as she
asked :

"Would it not relieve thee if
Sally and I were to 'tend the
baby ? " then glancing at my
company, "the children, I mean,
while thee lies down on mother's
bed."

My eyes filled with tears at the

thoughtfulness of these strangers. I had never known anything about " Quakers " before.

The baby was ready enough to exchange Bridget's charms for the dainty little ladies', and I clasped each of his small hands in Debby's, but instantly she transferred one-half her treasure to sister Sally, who turned demurely, and said :

" Thank thee. We will watch over him, and presently, if thee thinks best, I can give him some milk."

They had not quite reached the garden when Johnny burst forth. In great wrath he was indeed.

" Do they fink I am a baby ! " he roared out. " Get my cap, I want to go on the boat again ! "

" On the boat, Johnny ! "

He colored, and remembering his terror, revenged himself upon me by saying :

" I s'pose the reason they calls
me chillen is 'cause they's such
ole womans demselves ;" and having flung his parting shot he
walked off with great dignity.

A moment later he was lunch-
ing superbly from cold chicken
and apple tart out of the " 'ole
womans' " basket ! Such is mortal man !

Although I felt inclined to decline my little neighbor's invitation
to " lie down on mother's bed," it
was a great help to me to have
the baby so well cared for, and
Bridget's stout arms ready to
stretch and nail carpets. Down
they went rapidly, and was it the
fresh breeze from the ocean, wafted
through the pine trees, or was it
the glass of rich Jersey milk that
toned me up to such a cheery con-
dition that, when Jerry's step
sounded on the gravel, I rushed

to meet him, singing " Home, Sweet Home " ?

The good man was delighted with my progress, and especially with my report of the lovely little neighbors, which I lingered over.

" And where are they now, Kittie ? "

" Let us go quietly out to the garden and see, for I am sure I do not intend to impose on good nature by giving over baby entirely to them."

The tall drooping willow tree in the grass plot sheltered a lovely group. Baby mine, sound asleep in the big clothes basket, was snugly tucked up and protected by the little ladies, attended by that fickle youth, Master Johnny. His squeaky voice was plainly heard explaining the mysteries of Cat's Cradle and Wood Sawyer.

But in a moment more he called wildly :

"Aint that a big snake on the baby?" His companions sprang forward hurriedly, but the vicious boy only replied, "April Fool." The two girls hung their heads and colored. I held my breath. I could not believe they did not understand the joke. It was only an instant, and then Sally, laying her soft hand on stupid little Johnny's head, said in the silvery voice, so low and clear :

"Dear, could thee not just as well say 'Fourth Month Dunce'?"

PAMELIA TEWKSBURY'S
COURTSHIP.

PAMELIA TEWKSBURY'S
COURTSHIP.

N a certain section of Central New York the contour of the hills forms a remarkable resemblance to a huge *pitcher*, and by this name the region has long been known.

A few years since my husband and I, with a young son, took a delightful outing through that locality. Having our own horses and carriage, we made a very leisurely journey, aiming always for a comfortable resting place at night, and bearing away with us each morning a hamper containing luncheon for ourselves and a

bag of oats for the ponies. Thus
equipped, we traversed the distance to our next lodging according to our daily whim ; picnicking
at noon, in true gypsy fashion,
beneath some pine trees, or beside
a rippling stream ; turning from
coffee and sandwiches to a delicious course of " Humorous
Sketches," or a siesta upon pine
boughs.

Many comical adventures had
we. It was difficult to convince
the country people, who often
stopped to chat with us, that this
was recreation. They invariably
demanded a legitimate reason for
such unusual proceedings, and
more than one inquiring visitor
searched the light vehicle for some
wares that he had " made sure "
we were peddling.

Genuine offers of hospitality
were not wanting, and many a

pedestrian found a seat in the comfortable little carriage.

It so happened one morning that my husband was somewhat bewildered by the conjunction of several roads, and seeing in advance of us a sturdy figure moving forward at a good pace we hurried to overtake it. At the sound of approaching wheels, and the words "My friend, can thee tell me just where *Pitcher* lies?" a genial countenance was turned toward us.

"Wal, I reckon, this here," indicating the abrupt hills just before us, "is the handle. What part be ye looking fer?"

He had a ruddy face, very grizzly as to beard, and when he removed his weather-worn hat his smooth, bald crown, with a fringe of white curls, seemed an unfit accompaniment for the twinkling eyes of deep blue—such eyes as one sometimes sees in babies, wholly undimmed by care or tears.

"Why, I really don't know," laughed my husband; "I was directed to Hosmer's Inn."

"Oh, ho! that's atwixt the nose and the swell. Now ye are smiling, and well ye may; but just step out here and ye can see that God A'mighty shaped a perfecter pitcher out of them hills than most men can turn on a wheel— no, ye can't drive nigh to this stump, and that's whar yer woman wants to stand."

He helped us all to alight, gave me his hand as I climbed to the top of the stump, and pointed with his thumb to a rise of ground far in the rear.

"That thar's the rim, being what the pitcher ought to rest on if the Lord had sot it on end."

There was no possible irreverence in his tone. " Hereabouts," a rolling section nearer us, " is the swell. Just across Bub's left shoulder lies the nose, and here right for'ard is the beginning of the handle. Foller it—see it curves jest so."

It was very plain, and we all expressed our complete understanding of the " lay of the land."

" There is jest four p'ints where you can see the whole figger to onct. Here, by this hick'ry stump ; yander, north of the nose ; south of them pines ye see, and kinder back of the rim. Them's all, but it's worth a journey—and I take it ye are travelers—to see how darned perfect the thing is. Looked to right, it couldn't be beat ; and I reckon, somehow, it's about so with the most of God A'mighty's doin's—

ef we look to 'em *right* they're about perfect, that's all there is of it."

My husband thanked the old man cordially and invited him to ride with us if his route lay that way.

"Wal, now, I don't care ef I do, squire. Ye hev the speech of the Quakers and them's mighty good folk, and it haint often nowadays that I get behind two such spankin' roans as them be. Nor," as he clambered into the front seat, "nor nigh so sensible a looking woman—yer wife, maybe?"

"Yes; this is my wife and son."

"It's a darned good thing to hev yer wife with ye, along in life. I haint never had one yit," he added evasively.

We all smiled, but the old man didn't notice it. My husband spoke of the crops, of the fine air and good water. Our visitor answered in monosyllables. At last, pointing to a white gleam in the distance, he said, almost gleefully :

" Now, thar's a woman livin in that house, that I cal'late to call my wife one o' these days ; but time an't come yet."

" How so ? " asked I, rather hastily, I fear, for I scented a romance.

"Wal, it's a long story, but ef ye an't amiss I'd jest as lief tell it. We're mor'n six miles from Hosmer's." And with this little introduction the story proceeded.

" It was in 1846 that I first come to the nose. Our farm lay afar off to the rim—a little mite further. But our deestric wa'n't a-goin' to keep no school that winter ; so I up and asked father ef I dassent go off somewheres and get a job o' chores fer my board, and so

git one more term of schoolin'.
He hadn't no objections, and
kinder thought it over, and spoke
about Deacon Hinman at the nose
being laid up with *teesick* and
reckoned how he might want me.
So I packed my big red han'ker-
cher full o' traps and socks and
shirts, and away I come. I can
see myself now a-bobbin' up and
down this very lane. It wa'n't
worked by team then, and it was
full o' yaller-rod and spikenet, for
it had been an awful pretty fall.
So I, like a boy—and I love to
pick 'em yit—hung a posy bed
around my neck, and clean forgot
it when I knocked at the deacon's
side door. And what do ye
think? The durndest prettiest
gal up and opened it. I never
was so took back. I allers knowed
Deacon Hinman hadn't no
darters ; and there she stood and

me a-meachin', till all at once she said :

" ' A-peddlin' posies ? '

" Then my feelin' came back, and I answered her quick : ' Do you like 'em ? '

" And she took 'em, and was a-turnin' away as red as a piny herself when I recollected the deacon's teesick. So I stepped in the room and sot down on the settee, and says I : ' How's the deacon ? '

" ' He's abed,' says she.

" ' Got a man around ? '

" ' Ef we haint it's none o' your business. I'm man enough to tell ye that, and if ye haint got nothin' better to do than to sass folks and string posies 'round yer neck, I'd thank ye to git up and go.'

" I do not know as I ever heard Pamely Tewksbury say so much to onct in all my days since, fer she a'nt no talker; but, land's sake, didn't she skeer me, and didn't she look purty! I kinder shook all over, so I scarce got tongue to tell her who I was and what fetched me. She was ashamed enough then; I see it in her eyes, but she didn't never tell me. No, sir. That a'nt her way.

"The deacon's wife came in jest then, half a-cryin', for the cow had kicked her, and it didn't take long afore we struck a bargain, and in the evenin's she told me all about the deacon's teesick and her rheumatiz; but the only thing I could remember was that the gal was the deacon's niece come to live with them, and her name was Pamely.

"My! how that winter flew by. I don't reckon I l'arned a great deal to school, but I knew jest how many sticks of wood het the

stove up right to bake, and how
to plan to git time fer the churn-
ing Saturdays, and to turn out the
wash-water Monday nights fer a
gal who never said tire—but I
couldn't a-bear to see them little
arms a-liftin' so.

"Summer time come, and the
deacon wa'n't no better, and father
said how I'd better stay and hire
out for hayin'. I was a powerful
worker then—I can mow my swath
pretty reg'lar now—and I was a
powerful big eater, too ; but there
wa'n't no lack of vittles. The
deacon was allers a good provider,
and Pamely was a rare cook."

Here he paused, and turning toward the white speck, now grown
into a distinct homestead, he said
gravely :

"Ef ye was to put up there this
very day, and no one a-knowin'
of yer comin', *she'd* set ye afore

as good a meal at an hour's notice as ever Hosmer sot for two dollars and a half a day." Then the story went on.

"At first I used to talk to Pamely some, but after a while every time I tried to speak somethin' crammed in my throat, and it got to be so that I dassent try to talk. Evenin's I jest sot and whittled mush-sticks out of white pine, till she bu'st out one night, and says she : " S'pose you think I'm goin' to spile my mush every time with a new tastin' stirrer." And she laughed till she had to go out the room ; but what did I care ef she used them stirrers fer kindlin' ? I'd had my luck lookin' at her fingers fly a-sewin' or a-knittin', and I've got a pair of double blue and white streaked mittens now that she made that winter. It went along so fer 'bout

three year and more. I don't
think I keered much fer time. I
jest wanted to be a-earnin', winter
and summer, and that was what
it had come to, fer the deacon
didn't git much better, and the
wimmen folks couldn't git along
without me very well. They do
say now I'm dreffle handy; and
so long's Pamely set store by me,
I was all right. I declare to
goodness, I clean forgot there was
another young man in Pitcher but
me! But I had to wake up to it,
arter all, and I've wished a thousand times I had waked up
sooner.

"Pamely went off on a visit to
her folks, and when she come
back, onexpected like, a feller
fetched her. When I see him
a-liftin' her outen the sleigh I felt
like a-heavin' a claw-hammer at
him; but when he turned round,

and I saw what a putty-face he was, says I to myself, 'Pshaw!' Several times that winter he come, and set and set, and onct I got up and was a-goin' up the kitchen stairs when I felt somethin' in my heel. I sot down on the top step and pulled my stockin' off, a-lookin' fer a tack or perhaps a broke-off needle, when all of a sudden the door was ajar and they hadn't spoke a word afore I heard Jim Whiffles say : 'I knowed a feller as went a-courtin' one gal fer a whole year.'

"'P'r'aps,' said Pamely.

"'And she didn't chuck him off neither.'

"'S'pose not.'

"I tell you I listened close after that, but there was not a sound until Jim shove his chair and got up to go and she took the candle to the outside door, and then she come in and went right off to bed.

"Next mornin' I looked at her sharper'n ever but I couldn't see a shadder on her cheek. She was jest as bloomin' and as quiet as ever, and I knowed she cared more fer my leetle finger than fer the whole of Jim Whiffles' body.

"Next time he came it was near New Year's and he sot a big red apple plump in her lap ; but she did not so much as say 'thankee.' I thought she kinder of turned toward me, as much as to say, 'Ef ye had done it, all right.'

"'But I didn't *know*, and I reckoned I needn't begrudge Jim an evenin's lookin' at her. So I off to bed ag'in. I was thinkin' how mean I had been about lis-tenin' on the stairs, when up through the big stovepipe hole come these words, jerked out as usual : ' I think sometime there's goin' to be a weddin' up to our meetin'-house.'

" 'Like as not.'

" ' And I reckon Jim Whiffles is goin' to pay the dominee.'

" ' Likely.'

" That was all. My heart beat so I thought they must hear it, so I covered my head with the bed clothes, and in five minutes more he went away, callin' out as he drove off, ' Good-night ! '

" I did not sleep much, but I kep' up a thinkin' ; and at last I made out that nobody'd be such a fool as to ask a woman to have him that way ; and it must be Jim felt kinder sneakin', arter visitin' of her, and let her know he was a-goin to marry Ary Edwards that I had heard tell he went with. So I was comforted ag'in.

" It wa'n't more'n two weeks

afore I was took down with a fever·
Pamely nursed me night and day,
and every time I see her I said to
myself, 'Jest the first time I've
got strength to walk to the dominee's house we'll be made happy.'
Dear little soul ! What a good
supper she laid on the table the
night I was so tired out with doin'
of the milkin', havin' done nothin'
fer so long.

" ' Ezra,' she says, and her face
flushed up; ' Ezra eat. I've
cooked it fer you.'

" I wanted to blurt right out then
that I loved her, but I didn't.

" I had to tuck myself up mighty
early, for I was clean beat out,
and I declare fer it, but I was jest
fallin' into a doze like when I
heard Jim Whiffles come. Pamely
wa'n't done the dishes, so she
clattered away, and at last sot
down to knittin'. Nary one spoke

much, only to tell a word or two about the snow storm that was a-brewin'. And I was comforted ag'in, but it was short measure. When the clock had struck nine Jim got up, and while he was puttin' on his top coat I heard him say :

"'Pamely, I was a-tellin' ye last time I was here about Jim Whiffles paying the preacher?'

"' Jest so.'

"' And you was the gal that the dominee told to love and obey her man.'

"' Jest so.'

"I was breathless ! Was there nothin' more to come ? I had almost made up my mind that Jim was gone, when I caught the sound of a very decided smack. Good Lord forgive me, but I fought with the devil that night !

"Pamely and Jim Whiffles was

made one April 6, 1850. He fell heir to some property, and she got a thousand dollars when her uncle died, and a couple thousand more—in land—when Mrs. Hinman went off. So things prospered with them. He was hardworkin' kind of a putterer, but she was a master hand to save, and them children all was like her—smart as a steel trap.

"Eight years come next Tuesday Jim Whiffles died. I didn't need a second lesson—Lord A'mighty knows how hard it come to me onct! and I had loved Pamely right straight through. So, jest six months arter Jim was laid away I made a kind of an errant up to her house, and the very minnit I see her, it all came over me so I couldn't help it, and I screeched right out :

" ' Pamely, hev me ; do, fer goodness sake, say yes ! Don't you know I allers wanted ye ? '

" She turned 'round, and her eyes was a-flashin' when she answered :

" ' *Allers?* And lived in the same house nigh onto four years ? You had first chance, and now you come whinin' afore Jim's cold.'

" I sneaked off. I thought the Lord was ag'in me this time, but I jest couldn't give her up. I kep' right on goin'. All the children one arter another, has married and done well, and she boosted 'em all.

" Last Sunday I was over there ag'in, and, somehow, I thought she kind o' squeezed my hand at meetin' ; so I swelled up, and says I, ' Pamely, is Jim cold ? '

" And she answered back, ' Yes.' "

SOME ANTE-BELLUM LETTERS FROM A QUAKER GIRL.

.

SOME ANTE-BELLUM LETTERS FROM A QUAKER GIRL.

Ninth Mo., 27th.

MOTHER DEAR: When first thy loved face faded from view as our carriage left the crooked lane, my tears were inclined to flow, but Uncle Joseph has much of dear father's gentle manner, and he sought to turn my attention to the objects around us.

I will not pause now, to tell thee about the pleasures and pains of the journey, for my poor head ached sadly ere we reached Boston, but with all the interests that

surrounded my first long ride in
the railroad cars, I could not forget that I was going among com-
parative strangers, and leaving
the dearest spot on earth. I want
now to give thee a glimpse, if I
can, of the life here, and ask
whether or not thee approves of
the course I am pursuing.

It was quite dark when we got
to Uncle Joseph's house, and I
think I had a little fear of meeting
his wife, whom I can scarcely call
"Aunt" without an effort, so different is she from the simple women that I love. Her very first
greeting disturbed me, it was so
extravagant, and as full of em-
braces as if she had always known
me; but she was very kind when
she learned that my head ached,
and supported me tenderly to my
chamber, where she helped me
undress, and then with her own

hands, although they have several domestics, brought me a bit of toast and tea. I was sorry to disappoint her but I could not taste it, and she exclaimed petu-lantly, yet I may have mistaken the tone :

" Bless me, child, you are too young to have whims—and it is my duty to see that you keep the roses in your cheeks, or where will the lovers be ? Sit up now, and eat your supper."

I am afraid I betrayed the as-tonishment I felt, but, dear mother, *thee* could never speak thus, and— I did *not* eat the toast !

Next morning I was out in the garden marveling over the won-drous beauty of their surroundings, when Uncle Joseph came to look for me. His is a very sweet spirit, and I may be wrong, but there is pity in my heart for him.

Not that Aunt Élise (as she calls
it, although I should pronounce it
Eliza) does not try to do her duty
by him, but that her education
has given her false standards.

She was surprised to see me at
breakfast, and asked why I had
not called " the maid " to help me
dress. I replied that I needed no
one, and that thee and father believed that it was best to wait
upon ourselves; then she held up
her finger glistening with jewels,
and said :

" Tut, tut ! I fear we have a
rebel to deal with, and rebels are
never attractive. No, no, *ma petite* (which means little one), the
maid *must* assist you. She is from
Paris, and knows the *art* of dressing, which country girls know
nothing about, and I want to send
you home with a lover and a trous-
seau, and that could *never* be if

you comb your curls out, and wear a gray frock."

I believe she means to be kind to me, and is not at all disagreeable, even though I cannot seem pleased.

Well the day passed quickly by, for I was charmed with their green lawn running down to the riverside, and a little hedge of white hawthorn, that I am sure would delight thee. Toward evening aunt invited me to drive into the city with her and bring Uncle Joseph home. They do not have dinner until seven o'clock, which seems very late to me ; but about one, or a little before, we have a nice meal which I thought was dinner, until I was told to call it lunch. Aunt herself says it is breakfast.

The roads are so pretty, fine houses on every hand. It only

seems to me that there is an air of extravagance, which I deprecate, for there seem to be no small and unpretentious homes, until the city is reached, and there everything is so dreary! I am sure I should get lost very easily, for Boston's streets are as crooked as Philadelphia's are straight. I said to aunt that I should hardly dare for some time to come to town alone, and she answered :

"Never, I trust. It is highly improper for a pretty young girl to go out without an attendant."

I am sure *thee* never thought thus. Perhaps she was but trying to play upon my vanity.

I think the neighborhood must be a pleasant one just about Uncle Joseph, for yesterday a number of persons called, and spoke kindly to me. Toward four o'clock one of the young women asked aunt's permission for me to accompany her in a walk by the river. Soon after we left the house we came upon a group of young men, and my companion explained to them that she had succeeded in getting me away from my guardian, and then she gave me the names of the party, and I was surprised to know that two of them belonged to the old and respected families of A. and H. It seemed strange to mingle with the descendants of revolutionary times, and perhaps I expressed a little of the awe I felt, when I acknowledged their presence.

Thee has often told me that the Lord is no respecter of persons, and warned me against doing honor to anything mortal. Perhaps I have received a severe lesson, for I soon found that this was a premeditated excursion on the water, and there was a deal of laughter over the ease with which Anna W. had outwitted my aunt. Thee can imagine my discomfiture, both at finding myself in a false position and also at the discovery of their willingness to engage in deceit. Oh, mother, how have the mighty fallen! When I became conscious of the whole situation I said, just as I would have said to thee :

"If there is any doubt about my aunt's willingness to have me go with you, I must go back at once." And can thee believe it ? *they laughed*, and off the boat started.

Of course there was nothing to do but make the best of it. I tried to talk to young A. about his famous great-grandfather— but he seemed not to know much

about him, and when I spoke of
his nobility of character, the
young man looked bewildered,
and said if there had ever been
anything of that kind in the family,
it had died out.

I began to think so, too, as the
afternoon went on—for he puzzled
me greatly. All of these young
men are being educated at Harvard College, yet they did not ap-
pear to regard their opportunities
as unusual, and their references to
the professors were not respectful.
Edward H. inquired whether I
read French and on my saying
yes, he at once asked me if I had
a good pony—and I told him I
did not ride on horseback at all,
which seemed to amuse them
greatly, and Anna afterward explained that a *pony* was a transla-
tion—a key of the whole lesson
which the teachers do not expect

them to use, but which nearly the entire class possess.

We talked about the matter a little, and I said I should not think one could learn anything thus, and Edward H. replied " *That* is not what we go to Harvard for ! "

How strange it sounded ! And yet it was not so distressing to me as the discovery that these young men have absolutely no interest in anti-slavery movements. They talked about Garrison and Phillips as fanatics, and said " This meddling with other people's concerns is a very dangerous business."

I ventured to ask " And was it not ' meddling ' to throw the tea overboard."

But they said I was getting too deep for them. And then F. A. told me that only a very insignificant part of Boston people re-

spected the Abolitionists. This
new party they admitted has an
anti-slavery wing, but that it
must be clipped or we shall have
trouble. " Trouble " I cried—and
I admit, mother dear, that I talked
perhaps, more than I ought—" how
can a man rest easy without troubling the public conscience about
the poor slaves." A. tried to
show me that the best way to
eradicate slavery is to be on good
terms with the slaveholders, and
have no concern for the black
man, who is only an animal—I
think he said—after all, and when
it proves itself a failure in a business sense, as he admitted it must
be, then slavery will die out !

Not a spark of humanity about
him, not a thought of God's suffering children, only a fear of
disturbing business relations with
a rich section ! My heart stood

almost still with astonishment. Here in Boston, where I had looked for the broadest humanity and the clearest intelligence, here on the lips of the descendant of a great patriot were words of cowardice and self-seeking !

When at last the boat turned about, and the young men gave Anna W. and myself lessons in rowing, we came again to the little landing, and there on the bank stood aunt in search of us.

I felt mortified, and would have explained only that I could not reproach others, and I expected her to reprimand me, but lo ! she only shook her finger and said :

" Well, girls will be girls, and even a pretty Quakeress is not proof against temptation." How I wanted to tell the whole story ! But, mother dear, I did not. Was I wrong ? And the young men went away and my cheeks burned as aunt called after them, " I know you will want to see those roses again."

Good-night dear, dear mother.

Tenth Mo., 30th.

MY DEAR MOTHER: I know thee will not feel it to be wrong for me to tell thee of my trials as well as my pleasures, for thee has taught me that nothing is too small a matter to lay before our
. Heavenly Father, and in many respects I am puzzled by the new life I am leading here. Particularly do I regret having to think, and even to dwell upon, questions concerning money. That is, as thee has said, a necessity of our physical being, but must ever be relegated to the background in our thoughts. Uncle Joseph has asked me several times already

whether my purse was not empty, but although I have answered with a laugh that I did not see the bottom yet, I feel that I have been a little lavish, and of course I cannot permit another to purchase for me the luxuries which my pleasure-loving heart alone demands.

If thee wishes thee may send me some more, but should it prove inconvenient to do so, merely mention such to be the case, and I will absent myself from those excursions that are likely to be expensive.

I have been much mortified more than once already, by Edward H. or F. A. paying where I am concerned.

The first time this occurred was the day we sailed in the harbor. There were car fares, and boat tickets to be purchased, and I awaited Anna W.'s movement, before getting out my purse. To my surprise she said nothing about it, and the young men bought everything for us all. I estimated the cost at about a dollar apiece, which thee sees is quite an item when figured for four. So at the close of the day, for we had lunch and all, I spoke to Edward about it. We were walking at the time, and he stopped and laughed so immoderately that I was hurt. Perceiving this, he turned and taking my hand, said gently : " Do not deny me this pleasure. Oh, if I could always do it for you ! Your gratitude is so sweet."

What does thee think he meant, mother dear ? I was so perplexed by his speech that I was almost glad when Anna and F. A. turned to ask the cause of the laughter.

But how thoughtful Edward was not to expose me to others' merriment, for he turned the talk in another way immediately.

Was it not right and womanly in me to offer to pay the expense I had incurred? I want thy opinion, for I think it was, only, from his manner and that of Anna before, I fear such is not the custom; but I shall greatly hesitate to place myself under similar circumstances again.

It was with this thought in mind that I declined to go with them the next Seventh day. Everyone thought I was sick, and aunt began to imagine that I had looked pale all day! I denied feeling poorly, and was beginning to get embarrassed, when Edward H. walked to the window and asked me to come and see a peculiar cloud. This drew away the attention of the others and he said very gently :

" That cloud is no more peculiar than the one which has arisen between us, and it does not threaten half the harm." Then he went on to tell me that he suspected the reason of my refusal, and asked me to consider whether I would not like to do some small favor for him. I replied " Certainly." " Then," he said, " never speak of money where I am concerned, again. I have much more than I need, and I could not spend it in any manner that could both profit and please me more than by taking you about this region. Consider, too, the favors our family have had from your uncles."

Was it not kindly done ? And too, does thee not agree with my opinion that it *sounded* like Friends'

teaching? I shall await thy judgment impatiently—but I went
with him.

Another curious thing has happened too. I expect thee will
laugh at the many adventures that
befall me. On Sixth-day evening
it rained very hard, but Uncle
Joseph had tickets for a concert, which they wished very
much that I should hear. I
thought it would be discour-
teous to decline, although I
do feel that vast sums are thus
frittered away, which might benefit the poor. To my surprise
aunt said I should wear a wool
frock, as we were not going to
take the horses on account of the
rain, but would be driven only to
a point where we can meet the
horse railroad, which is often a
very great convenience.

Notwithstanding the bad

weather there was a large
number of persons present in the
hall. I cannot pronounce judgment upon the concert, for I have
no knowledge concerning these
things. One lady who sang
seemed to have, naturally, a sweet
voice, but it was overstrained, and
the long drawn notes were quite
offensive. I am sure, however,
that the audience was satisfied,
and uncle and aunt have re-
peatedly signified their delight,
and hope to have another opportunity to listen to her. I did my
best to express my thanks for the
kindness in taking me, without
mentioning my distaste for such
entertainments, but my aunt suspected me, and laughingly said " I
believe you are sleepy, child.".
And in truth I was! However, I
was soon wide enough awake.
We missed the car we had hoped

to gain, and had to wait in a little room, nearly half an hour. All sorts of people were there. More than once aunt said wearily, " I hate these mixed crowds, and I shall not let my pity for the horses inconvenience us like this again."

For my part I was quite interested in watching the people. Just as the car came there was a new throng, and we found it necessary to separate our seats. Indeed uncle, with many other gentlemen, was forced to stand the whole way. Just in front of me was a group of Harvard students, and the moment of starting added to their numbers some who were evidently under the influence of liquor. One of them was a very young fellow, neatly dressed and with a sweet expression of countenance, but, mother dear, he was really intoxicated. He staggered into the door, and leaning against the post actually *snored.* Many of the persons present laughed, but the sight was very sad to me, and a nice young man, tall and straight as Cousin Benjamin, who was close beside me, said, no doubt observing my distress : "This troubles you." I answered : "Indeed it does ; think of the boy's parents ! " He assented, and remarked that the lad was evidently a " Freshman "—that is, a newcomer at college—for that is what they are called in their first year.

"And what will become of him when he gets out of the car ?" I asked, for I could plainly see that the poor boy was too much befogged to find his way home alone.

" If he has no friend with him,

a policeman may get hold of him."

"How terrible," I said, with some warmth perhaps.

"I suppose," continued the young man after quite a pause, "that I *could* take him to his room if he has any way to indicate where that is, or to mine until morning, if that will relieve your mind."

I supposed I brightened up a good deal at this, and I urged it upon him, but he did not positively promise, for he quite shocked me by bending close to me and saying almost in a whisper:

"If I do, it will be done for your sake, remember, and one good turn deserves another, so tell me where you go to church."
I was so much surprised that for a moment I could not answer; then he repeated his request, but the car stopped with a jerk that it usually

has, and my uncle and aunt signified that we were to get out.

The carriage was waiting, but we had scarcely made ourselves comfortable, when my aunt exclaimed :

" Sallie, I do believe you were talking to those strange men in the car. What will you do next to astonish me ? "

I saw my uncle closely regarding me, and with a more severe expression than I had ever seen him wear, but I could not believe I had done wrong to take a humane interest in the tipsy boy. So I told them all about it—except that I did not repeat the foolish speech of the tall young man ; it was not worth remembering.

My uncle's face softened as he heard me out, and he patted my aunt's plump hand and said, smiling at me :

" I guess she means well always, Élise. Customs differ, you know."

But I do not think she regarded it so lightly, for she sighed heavily, and on First day when I stood ready to accompany her to meeting—I mean church—she came into the entry leading to my room, and began :

" Sallie, child, I beg you not to talk to the minister between prayers," and then she suddenly turned, took my cheeks between her hands and kissed each of them, saying rather wildly I thought, " But I declare, *ma petite*, you are pretty enough to turn the head of any male creature."

She is a strange person ! So full of moods—and tenses I might say—but very very kind to thy simple Sallie.

Of course thee understands

that I gave no clew whatever to
the place of worship where I was
in the way of going.

Nevertheless, last First - day
night, when I walked to the "Ves-
per Service," I think it is called, in
company with our young friends,
Anna, F. A., and Edward H., whom
should I see standing in the vesti-
bule, but the tall young man ! I
assure thee I wanted to ask him
how it fared with the poor tipsy
boy, but I dared not, particularly
after what aunt had said to me.
Still, I could not be unmindful of
his presence all through the hour,
for he followed us into the room
and sat just where he could see
us all the time. I resolved to
banish worldly thoughts, but I am
afraid I did not, so that I grew
very uncomfortable, and was glad
when the end came, but even then
I was pained by Edward asking

me where in the world I had met Jack D. I answered that I was not acquainted with any person so named.

"Well, that *is* a puzzle," he said, "for he has been in Europe six months, and this is the first time I have laid eyes on him, yet I could have declared [he really said *sworn*, but I don't think he means evil by it] that he recognized you as we went in."

I had to say something, so I inquired what class "Jack D." belonged to, and this was his response:

"Great Jehosephat! Jack D. is the swellest senior on record. If once you get into his cave he sports his oak, and treats you like a nabob."

The Harvard vernacular is sometimes hard to translate!

But I am burning too much
gas.

Affectionately,

THY DAUGHTER.

Eleventh Mo., 3d.

MOTHER DEAR : Anna W. and
I have just returned from what was
in many respects a most interest-
ing excursion, and yet it had its
dark side.

Almost immediately after I had
written to thee last week, aunt
carried me to town and insisted
upon my choosing several nice
garments. It was wholly unnecessary, for my wardrobe, thee knows,
was very comfortable, and I did
not care to be under so great obli-
gation to her, but I found that to
do otherwise would hurt her feel-
ings, so I chose, very reluctantly, a
white merino that she said I must
have to wear in the evening, and

aunt herself selected a pretty pale blue silk. It seems gay for me, but she has promised that it shall be made in a plain way. I am afraid, however, that her ideas and mine concerning those things will not agree. Lastly, she bought a gown and cloak of a heavy texture, and trimmed with beautiful gray fur. There is a muff too. I submit rather than enjoy taking so much, pretty as the things are. I am not certain that I can trust my pride, which gets the better of poor mortals so soon, but thee told me to do as nearly as possible without troubling my conscience, as aunt desires, therefore I shall wear the expensive garments with less thought of the unnecessary outlay than I otherwise could. Uncle Joseph says the color of the fur is the only thing that reconciles me to the purchase.

Indeed I am ashamed to tell thee that the making of each dress—for I saw the bill—has cost about seven dollars !

Well, I will add to this worldly record, that when the cloak and muff came home, there was also a round hat, with a long soft feather on it ! *Of course*, I could not be comfortable in that, and as it is quite a new thing for me to wear aught but a bonnet, aunt was persuaded by dear Uncle Joseph to substitute a bit of ribbon and a band of the fur for the feather, but I almost wish thee could have seen it just as I first did, it was beautiful !

The young men come home from Harvard College every Seventh day at noon, and we mostly go together, Anna W., F. A., Edward H., and myself for a drive or a walk. It is getting rather cool for boating. Aunt seems to find it quite "*proper*" for four of us to be together. She says (I hate to tell thee this) that either of the boys would be a very desirable "parti!" Such suggestions drive away all the pleasure that would come from their companionship, so I try to turn a deaf ear when she approaches the subject.

To-day we went to Nahant, a beautiful rocky beach, where there is a large hotel in summer, and many charming seaside homes. One of the cottages is owned by a relative of F. A. and is still open, so we agreed to accept an invitation to dine.

It was so cool that I wore my new gown and hat, but they all had so much to say concerning their perfections and becomingness that I felt pained, and told them so. Edward H. was quite serious over it and asked me *why* I should not enjoy knowing I had fine eyes, unusual hair, and a bright color. Of course I could only answer that if God had given me *honest* eyes and healthy color I was very glad, but that˙ I believed he did not wish me to think too much about them—and Edward said, " Well, you need not. We will do the thinking." So then I blushed more and more, but I managed to ask him not to do any more *talking* about it.

We left Uncle Joseph's at eight o'clock in the morning, F. A. driving his father's horses, which are very fleet. I never had a more exhilarating ride. The air was delicious and we were a long time directly by the ocean. Oh, I wished for thee continually ! Anna wanted to drive part way. So Edward got back in the seat with

me, and presently our conversation drifted into politics. Thee
knows I am no politician, and that
I adhere to the belief of Garrison,
that the Constitution of the United
States is a "Covenant with Hell,"
but I confess I am greatly interested in the Republican party. If
Charles Sumner is right in his
opinion of the Constitution, then
through political action we may
look for the final overthrow of
slavery, but Edward is not even a
Republican ! He says the very
foundations of our government
will be shaken if they elect their
president, and I am not sure that
he is wrong ! Let them be shaken,
and relaid say I. He calls me a
rebel, and warns me that if another
Anthony Burrs appears in Boston,
I may walk the streets in chains,
as a conspirator against the peace
and well-being of society. I can

see that he goes to greater length than he otherwise might, because he thinks it teases me.

I asked F. A. to what party he belonged, and he quickly answered, " The Know Nothings." I could not help joining in the laugh that followed, although it is a serious matter to me, and the levity with which these young men, of stanch old revolutionary blood, treat such questions astonishes me beyond measure.

Indeed I have as yet met no one whom I could characterize as other than " conservative." One evening I said this in the parlor, and aunt quickly answered that to be erratic was always unpopular, and young people cannot afford to forego the pleasures of society. So she begged me not to say much even though I felt a great deal.

No doubt she intended to do me a kindness by this warning, but the contrast between this teaching and thine, dear mother mine, brought tears to my eyes. I think Uncle Joseph must have observed them, for when aunt was called out of the room, he patted me on the head and whispered, " Next week I am going to give my little girl a treat. We will not talk about it now, but she shall see and hear some Bostonians who are *not* conservatives." I kissed him, and then we both laughed ; and when aunt came in again he proposed a game of authors, which we play very often. It is quite new, and I am sure they have learned it in kindness to me, since they have discovered that I do not play cards. Did I ever tell thee my experience on this matter ? It was soon after my arrival that

a party of friends came in to
spend the evening, and cards were
proposed. It seems that aunt is
a great card player—whist I believe they call it—and prides herself not a little on teaching it to
others. It needs a certain number
to perfect the game, and includ-
ing myself there was just enough
for two parties. When I found
how matters were I am afraid I
felt cowardly about avowing my
principles. It is so unpleasant to
make others uncomfortable, but I
did not hesitate long. I spoke
quietly to Uncle Joseph and asked
him please not to count me, as I
could not play. Aunt heard me
and answered before he had time
to do so : "Oh, that does not
amount to much. You shall be
my partner, and as you are sur-
prisingly quick to learn, I will
guarantee that another time you

can lead a game." I know my poor cheeks burned, but I had to tell her more. " Dear aunt," I said, " it is not that I am ignorant, for you are both ever ready to help me, but that I believe it is wrong." I wish thee could have seen the astonishment on her face. Her tone changed at once, and she spoke rather harshly, " Come, come, child, let us have no whims. How often do you have to be told that the judgment of your elders is enough. This is no concern of yours save to do as you are bid ; take your place." I am sure I do not know what would have followed—for I *certainly* could never have yielded and even for peace' sake touched the pasteboard that is connected in my mind with all that is low and of evil report. But our struggles are never forgotten, and a friend was raised

up. One of the ladies appealed
to her brother to know if he had
the new game in his pocket—
authors—and then very graciously
aunt permitted half of us to play
this very simple and innocent
amusement. Why is it to do right
sometimes costs so much trouble
to others? I think thee would
say : We cannot solve all the
problems of life ; this is one that
must rest with a higher intelligence than our own.

Uncle Joseph has just brought
me a card of invitation to a party
at the house of John B.'s mother.
A queer little dark woman full of
learning ! With the card was a
penciled note : " Our liberal entertainment will not take place until
the week following Thanksgiving." I suppose uncle wrote this,
rather than talk about it before
my aunt. But how sad it must

be for two really well-meaning people not to agree in their principles.

Dear mother, I have kept this letter until after the party in order to tell thee about it, but I am afraid neither of us will quite enjoy my relation of it.

In the first place aunt insisted upon dressing my hair and arranging some flowers about my blue silk frock. She is really an artist in those things, and with the help of the maid I scarcely knew myself! Forgive me, if I say I could but admire the creature they had constructed. And yet it made me cry, I looked like a stranger! I thought best not to say a word but to go just as I was, in order to please her. Every time I passed a glass I felt like an imposter! Dear Uncle Joseph drove with me in the carriage and came after me

at what *they* regard as an early
hour, eleven o'clock. On the way
he said, "Little girl, try and forget your furbelows, and next time
I will persuade aunt to let you go
in your simple white frock." So
I was comforted. And indeed I
tried hard to forget, but I could
not. People looked at me on every
hand, and I thought it must be
because it was as if I was trying
to be someone else than a Friend.
Then came another trial. There
was a large room with a linen cover
over the rich carpet, and dancing
going on. The musicians sat in
the upper hall, and supper was
served from ten on. I had no
sooner gone through with the
ceremony of various introductions,
than I was surrounded by young
men, who asked me to dance. I
suppose they did so out of kindness to a stranger, but Anna W.

helped me in my trouble, by saying "Yes" to each one that asked
me, and then I explained that
Friends did not think it right to
dance, and one young man made
us laugh heartily by saying :

"Why, I thought you were a
Quaker or a Shaker, or something
that dances all the time, even when
they go to church !" Did not that
show gross ignorance ?

The supper, too, tried me, for
everyone, almost without an exception, took a glass of wine ! Anna
told me it was a "light wine," but
that could make no difference to
me.

Edward H. was my escort, and
when I declined taking it, he put
his glass down untouched. I
thought it was very wise in him.
Perhaps the thought of its inju-
rious influence was new to him.
We did not talk about it, but half

a dozen times we were urged to drink. It really made me sad, for these young men are not proof, always, against temptation, and indeed I had reason to fear before I left, that the wine had affected one of them at least; for as I stood waiting to say Good-night, he asked if he might accompany me home, and when I told him uncle was coming for me, he added : " I do not blame him for trying to keep such a beauty to himself as long as possible ! "

During the evening a young matron living near here told me some of their friends had proposed to have a series of "sociables," meeting at their houses alternately, and wished me to join. I am sure it is very kind, although I do not know what sort of entertainments these are to be, but I thanked her and said I would ask aunt's permission, and to my surprise, as she threw my shawl about my shoulders, she stooped and kissed me, "Good-by for the present!" That is what they use here as the form of farewell.

THY LOVING DAUGHTER.

Eleventh Mo., 24th.

DEAR MOTHER: Oh, what a treat I have had! Nothing that Uncle Joseph could have done would have given me more pleasure than attending the Anti-Slavery Fair, held in Music Hall last week. I think thee cannot estimate aright the effort which it cost him, unless thee calls to mind all that I have told thee concerning the real relation of the business men of Boston to the comparatively small number belonging to the A. S. Society. Of course aunt knew about our attendance, although I doubt whether she had an invitation to join us, and she made merry continually over what she called our "escapade."

When I went upstairs to get my cloak, she called to me, "Girly, put on all your *outré* garments; you must look odd, or you will not be in harmony with your surroundings. Only *queer* people belong."

The entertainment began at half-past seven with a tea ; that is, small tables were scattered about, where one could sit down, and the ladies handed around tea and cakes. My pleasure began at once, for we had scarcely entered the hall, which, by the way, is *very* large, when we met Uncle Joseph's old friend, Daniel K. I had seen him before, and he told me how much I was like grandmother. So now, as soon as he saw us, he tucked my hand under his arm and bore me across the room, where, behind one of the tables sat a stout elderly woman, in a very queer cap. I have seen pictures like it, and does thee remember Elizabeth Jones, who did our laundry work one summer? She wore a similar one. It was not thin like thine, but rather heavy in texture, with a wide frill about the face. But the woman beneath it was very attractive. She had such bright eyes and a most winning smile.

She spoke with Friend Daniel, and I did not catch his words, but immediately she came around to us, stroked my hair and invited me to pour tea. Then someone else came and called her by name, and who does thee think it was? Lydia Maria Child. When I realized that I was helping the writer of those beautiful stories, I had to turn and look at her more closely and I could not help saying, " Did thee ever know David and Jonathan ? " We laughed together, and she seemed pleased that I had read her works. For an hour or more we waited on the cake and tea, and then Uncle Joseph took me over to the other side where articles were exposed for sale. I bought a few trifles, which uncle insisted upon paying for, but thee knows just about what Philadelphia fairs are, so I will not repeat. One thing however I must speak of. I selected a tiny package of visiting cards tied together with a bit of ribbon, and each one was inscribed with the name of a prominent Abolishionist written by himself. William Loyd Garrison, Wendell Phillips, Charles Remond, Stephen Foster, and so on. I thought I

should like to keep them until I
am old, and tell my children how
I came to have them. I also
bought a pocket pincushion with
alternate black and white pins.

Presently there was some music,
for which I did not care, and then
a gentleman announced Wendell
Phillips as a speaker. My! but
I wish thee had been there! Such
enthusiasm! and with good reason. I do not believe I ever saw
a finer looking man. He has a
little look of a man of the world,
but one forgets that as soon as he
opens his lips. Then came forth
no uncertain sounds, but genuine
thunderbolts of truth and elo-
quence. Oh, it was grand!
Uncle says he spoke over half an
hour, but it seemed short to me,
and as he left the platform I
sighed. Uncle Joseph inquired
what I would like next, and I an-

swered "Either Sumner or Emerson," and lo ! as if I had touched
a magic spring, *both* of them appeared. The former, thee is
aware, is not able to do duty, but
his magnificent presence was
enough, and he smiled down at
the audience with a great friend-
liness as he said he "wanted to
introduce Ralph Waldo Emerson."
Everybody laughed and cheered,
and the gentle philosopher spoke
only a little time, about human
rights and human wrongs. I was
much impressed by his manner,
which is that of one who solilo-
quizes rather than of an orator.
He is a great contrast in appearance too, to those who preceded
him—tall and slender, his head
bowing just a little, as if it was
heavy with great thought, but
there is not much fire about him,
and thee would undoubtedly like

him the better for it. He is very
genial, for I saw him talking and
smiling with all who approached.
I hear that he has a great rever-
ence for the *individual*, and looks
not for the foibles, but the majesty
of the man.

I asked Uncle Joseph if he
thought it would be right for me
to speak with William Lloyd Garrison, of whom dear grandfather
had so much to say, and I soon
found that the very name of my
good ancestor was a passport
everywhere in the room. I was
introduced to the Garrison young
people, three sons at least ; and
the mother asked me to come and
see her, which I should like to do,
but it is scarcely probable. I do
not wish to offend aunt's prej-
udices, unnecessarily, and my
visit there could be of no real
use.

I saw Elizabeth Peabody, who is trying to interest people in the kindergarten methods of teaching young children, by playing and talking with them, rather than through books, and it certainly seems a most reasonable system.

It seems to me now as if I had seen Boston, for the people who were at the Fair were the very people I have heard about, and read about all my life—the people indeed, whom *I* supposed constituted Boston, and yet outside their own circle, few know or care whether they exist. I am wrong. They have been raised up for a holy purpose, and if, as it seems, the busy mart is deaf to their entreaties for universal liberty, unconditional emancipation, the sin will lie at its own door should bloodshed follow.

I am afraid this meeting with

those in whom I am so much interested will rather spoil me for our everyday routine. It is pleasant enough, but it seems selfish to devote so large a share of time to one's entertainment. I sometimes long for active *work ;* but aunt says it spoils the domestics (servants is her word) to help them, and it spoils a " lady's hands "! I never heard thee complain in that way, and there are no dearer or daintier hands than thine, which are ready for pot or pan, needle or butter mold. Perhaps it is a little Pharisaical to thank God we are " not like other men," but I am thankful that I was sent into thy arms !

I have been tempted to say that I had a *complete* pleasure at the Anti-Slavery Fair, but as I was about to write it thus, a reminder came to me of *one* thing that I wanted and did not get, and that was a piece of *temperance mince pie ;* for I heard it said that there were such in an adjoining room, and much as I like pies, I have steadfastly declined tasting those that looked so nice at uncle's table, for I know full well they are made with a strong infusion of brandy.

We came out home by the horse railroad again, and I somehow could not help thinking about the poor tipsy boy and the tall young man, and strange enough, the latter got into our car ! I did not lift my eyes once, on the whole route, for he sat directly opposite me, and I thought it would be dis-courteous not to acknowledge his presence, and to do so would trouble my uncle. So I was espe-cially weary when we got out, and I thought the young man went on

further, but just as we stopped
he sprang up as though he had
been asleep and in hurrying out
he jostled me, and begged me to
excuse it. He has a fair voice,
manly, and direct, and—but what
does thee think? after he had
passed, there was a scrap of paper
lying on my muff! Perhaps I
ought to have thrown it away without reading, but I *did* want to
know about the poor lad, and so
I crumpled it up in my glove,
until I got into my quiet chamber,
and then I saw that it was a bit
torn from a newspaper border,
and beautifully written with a lead
pencil. It said: " I took him
home and have talked with him
since about the wrong he has
done. I think it will not happen
again."

Was it not kind in " Jack D."
to let me know in this way, with-

out intruding upon me, or even signing his name?

I intended to bring home the little cushion I bought at the fair, but when I told Edward H. all about it, he said that he would like a memento to recall what I have told him about the sin of slavery, which I really believe he had never been taught to consider. So I gave him the pinball.

I must tell thee about my French lessons next time. Aunt speaks with a fine accent, they tell me; and she thinks I have been well taught.

I wish I could kiss thy dear cheek. Farewell,

SALLIE.

PHILADELPHIA,
Fourth Mo., 26th.
MOTHER DEAR : Thy presence has been roundabout me through-

out the day, and I cannot sleep
until I have availed myself of this
poor medium, my pen, to convey
to thee some of the thoughts that
fill my mind.

Cousin Henry went with me to
attend the morning meeting at
Race Street, where we listened to
words of warning and words of
comfort from the lips of Friend B.
and Friend T., and I was quite lost
in meditation following the dis-
course of the latter, whose fine
voice I ofttimes fear has an influence over me that should only be
the result of his spiritual teaching.
Then Lucretia Mott arose and
spoke very acceptably, as she has
ever done, to me. Yet it was not
the words that fell from her lips
that so greatly affected me, it was
the memory of a strange scene
that I have recently witnessed
that endeared her to me, and it is

of this that I am anxious thee
should know.

On Second day, while we were
awaiting Cousin Henry at the customary dinner hour, a lad brought
in a note asking aunt to excuse his
non-appearance and begging her
to bring some friends and join
him at the office of the U. S.
Commissioner on Fourth Street
as soon after two o'clock as possible.

It seems that a colored man had
been claimed as a fugitive slave
by a Southerner staying in the
city, and this reaching the ears of
a prominent Abolitionist, a few
persons resolved to make a strenu-
ous effort to have the case pub-
licly tried.

Such, as thee knows, is not the
usual proceeding, for the poor
creatures are generally given over
to the hands of their taskmasters

with very little noise or show of justice.

The watchword was quickly passed, and when the case was opened the small room was densely packed and it was made evident to the commissioner that considerable excitement prevailed. He therefore judged it best to delay further trial until 2 P. M., at which hour the court would sit in the large hall just around the corner, by Independence Square, and it was there that aunt took me.

Friend J. and his wife, Elizabeth C. and two sons, and four or five other "plain bonnets and broad brims," entered the room about the same time that we did. A. L., whom thee remembers, was present and arranged comfortable seats for us, some having benches, others chairs, while a large table in the middle of the hall was sur-

rounded with the roughest looking
men I ever saw! They were
armed with pistols and bowie
knives and handled their weapons
too freely to make me comfortable.
And yet how cowardly I felt when
I glanced at the poor slave face so
full of terrible anticipation!

The room was fast filling up
with Southern sympathizers when
Lucretia Mott quietly took her
place beside the colored man, and
after speaking kindly with him
drew forth her knitting work! I
never saw anything so diabolical
as the countenances of the company about the table, as they com-
mented to each other upon her
appearance there. Evidently they
resolved to render her situation as
trying as possible, which, I assure
thee, they never failed to do during
the whole session.

Of course thee knows I had

never been in a court room before, and so I am afraid I shall not be able to give thee anything more than a very meager account of the regular proceedings. It seems that the identity of the slave had first to be proved, with the date of his escape. Then the poor man brought what testimony he could quickly gather as to his having lived near Lancaster for a greater length of time than his would-be owner asserted. The evidence was given under great difficulties because the strong Southern bias of the crowd broke forth in wild cries and oaths, whenever the adverse testimony came on. Sometimes the noise was deafening. The commissioner is a frail man of middle age, and by the way, a descendant of 'Friends. He made great exertion to maintain order, but frequently looked

as if he feared the result of inter-
ference.

Hour after hour went on. The
twilight had grown into darkness
and midnight finally drew near.
None of the anti-slavery party
had been allowed to leave the
room, or rather having left it, to
return. Everyone was getting
hungry, yet I think we all thought
especially of the good woman who
sat so calmly beside the not over
cleanly colored man, but I am
bound to add, with a group of
tried and true friends close around
her.

In one of the pauses loud voices
were heard outside, and a rush
toward the door gave us fear that
a measure was on foot to seize the
prisoner and carry him off under
the very eye of the law, but we
found the trouble arose from a
young man insisting upon being

allowed to enter with refreshments for Lucretia Mott. He was actually driven away by force, and only after a hazardous entry, by means of a water pipe and window, was he able to present the modest supper to her. Thee will not be surprised to know that she at once shared it with other Friends in attendance.

Soon after daylight the commissioner announced that the testimony had all been taken and he found himself too much fatigued to continue the sitting, therefore the court was adjourned until 2 P. M. of that day. I had grown very restless, as thee may imagine, and turning to aunt I said, "I scarcely dare breathe for fear the poor man must go back to his chains." A. L., who sat near, touched me lightly on the shoulder, and replied: "Prepare thy-

self calmly for the worst in life,
and thus thee will not be over-
whelmed when disaster comes,
and should the best be realized
thy joy will be proportion-
ate.".

I think I shall never forget his
remark. The whole scene is so
vivid before me. I cannot close
my eyes without seeing every
detail of the crowded room, dimly
lighted, and the shadowy figures
in the shady corners leaning anx-
iously forward to catch the expression as well as the words of an
earnest old black man, who was
questioned and cross-questioned
for hours on the witness stand.
I know, mother, that had it been
I, I should certainly have made
some mistake, but he did not get
greatly confused, only wandered
slowly over and over again in his
statements and settled down upon

what proved to be the absolute truth.

It seems he was a small gardener in the neighborhood where the prisoner worked, and had written down in his rough notebook the date of the stranger's arrival. This book was the only direct testimony in favor of freedom, for all the other witnesses became confused, or else exhibited clearly the falsity of their statements. As it turned out, the good, conscientious gardener had made a mistake in his date, and the commissioner suspected it, but as A. L. told us they could not go behind the written facts and we all thought he was, indeed, greatly harassed by the situation and was glad enough to be able " to give the prisoner the benefit of the doubt," which I suppose is a formal phrase that applies to

causes decided upon suspicious
evidence, and thee knows, it is
often said that English law leans
toward mercy.

Alas! that it should not always
be based upon justice! And,
mother dear, thee will recall here
a great deal that I have written
thee about the young men of New
England with whom I have been
thrown during the year. I cannot
bring myself back to the old
thought that I bore concerning
them. I expected the H. and A.
families were as eager for the
abolition of slavery as their fore-
fathers were to found a "free
and independent nation," and be-
hold! they jeer at Garrison and
Phillips and hesitate to do anything that will hurt Southern
pride.

Thee has ever taught me to
"judge not," yet I would that the

youth of distinguished patriot
families now enjoying every edu-
cational advantage at the great
seat of learning—Harvard College—might also feel the throb of
sympathy for the oppressed. But
we must turn back to the terrible
slave trial.

At times, toward dawn espe-
cially, when the men grew weary, I
suppose, the pistols were flourished
as if they were harmless things. I
drew very near to dear aunt once,
but she quietly pointed to Lucretia Mott, whose age required
rest, but whose motion betrayed
neither her weariness nor deep
concern. It was a relief when a
little before nine o'clock the
court was adjourned. It seems
there was some thought of at-
tempting a forcible capture of the
man on trial, but his anti-slavery
friends gathered close about him

and thus remained until he was in the hands of the officers of the law.

Of course we were very tired, but nothing of small importance could have kept us from rejoining the throng, for such it had now become, when court opened again that afternoon.

What is called the " argument " began as soon as order was established. First the lawyer on one side, a much disfigured man named B. B., tried to show that all the evidence was in favor of the slaveholder. That is, that the man claimed was really the escaped slave, and this being so, the commissioner ought to give him up. Then the other, G. E., made a most satisfactory response, stating that the only evidence to be relied upon was the gardener's account book, and that distinctly

showed the man to have been free
at the time he was said to have
run away. Oh, mother ! I wish
thee could have heard him.   I
know it is dangerous to allow
one's enthusiasm too great liberty,
but I never felt so well satisfied
with any speaker before.

At last it was over and a long
reading from the commissioner
closed the matter.   Even aunt, I
think, was in doubt how it might
end, until the very last sentence,
and then—although I did not ap-
prove of the sentiment—I could
not help a touch of sympathy with
a man near me who shouted ex-
citedly, " You have saved your
soul, commissioner ! "

Such excitement ! People shook
hands and cried and—the slave
had disappeared ! No one saw
him go, no one seemed to know
where he went, but aunt whis-

pered to me that it was all right, he was taken in charge by a friend and would be immediately out of harm's way. I think it was an hour before we could get down to the street, so thronged was the staircase, and everyone seemed happy over the result.

I am inclined to think my mind dwelt as much on the awful responsibility of the commissioner as upon the released man. How *can* one bind himself by an oath to serve a government that has made this iniquitous bond with the slaveholders ? I *almost* hope to learn later that this dreadful experience has led to the resignation of Commissioner L.

There was one other thing, mother dear, that gave me great joy. In the midst of the enthusiasm, someone seized my hand. I was not astonished at the movement for every heart seemed to be throbbing with sympathy and brother love, but I assure thee I was very happy when I lifted my eyes and saw bending over me the familiar face of Edward H.! What a fine face it is! And on this occasion burning with new-born devotion to principle! It is needless to say that he has since been to visit us, and that he is going to return to Pennsylvania during the summer and has kindly responded to my invitation to come to our home.

Thee cannot help loving him, I know, nor can dear father either, and you will both rejoice that— for Edward has so expressed it— through your simple Sallie's teaching a strong man has been led to see the enormity of our national sin, and pledged himself to leave no stone unturned toward its abolishment.

In firm affection, I remain

THY DAUGHTER.

N. B.—I think perhaps I ought to tell thee about a letter I have recently had from F. A. A kind letter, but with a tone of flattery that I do not quite like, nor, indeed, understand. He speaks as if I was much in his thought and —can it be, dear mother, that I gave him a wrong impression of my friendship? My cheeks burn as I write this, but it is delightful to know good Edward H. was thoroughly inspired—through my mere suggestion that these are serious times—to do a great deal of honest thinking. I shall be right glad to welcome him within our home!

UNCLE JOSEPH.

UNCLE JOSEPH.

NE of the prominent fig-
ures in our meeting
house for many years
was that of Uncle Joseph—for
thus was he known by the young
and old who frequented our religious gatherings.

He occupied the second seat in
the men's gallery—and it was with
him that the Elder shook hands in
sign that Friends should separate,
when it seemed likely that the
spirit would move no others to
utter gentle words of blessing or
stern warning against the wiles of
the tempter.

As children we regarded Uncle
Joseph in the light of a patriarch,

although I now know that his years, at the time of which I write, had scarce reached the limit of a half century.

He was a comely man, straight and tall, his smooth-shaven face beaming with good nature, and his soft blue eye lighted with sympathy, but he was not intellectual. Slow of movement and uncertain in expression, his hearers were often troubled to follow his excellent thought, and it was no uncommon thing for my parents to refer to his ministrations as being "labored." We had a consciousness, based perhaps upon accidental knowledge, that he was uncommonly well to do, and also that there was considerable feeling in the society that Sarah Sidney, with her clear insight and facile speech, would be a fit life companion for the good man.

But time wore on and there seemed
no likelihood of a realization of
this desire.

I can remember one occasion
when the subject really assumed
the importance that is usually
given to gossip, but it was so lov-
ingly and conscientiously touched
upon that I was greatly impressed.

My father and mother were in
the way of inviting many friends
to dine with them on monthly
meeting day. Quarterly meeting
brought even more persons from a
distance, and among the children
little unaccustomed duties were dis-
tributed. I was frequently desired
to remain for a time in the front
chamber and assist our women
visitors in removing their wraps
and adjusting the cap crowns that
often met with disaster beneath
the stiff bonnets. It was always
a pleasurable duty, for Friends

never forget the young, and as each one grasped my little palm, she did not neglect to speak an encouraging word.

On the occasion to which I have alluded, meeting broke up somewhat later than usual. I hurried home, warmed my chilled fingers, and ran upstairs, where a bright fire was burning on the hearth. I glanced about to see that the wood box was full, and looked out of the window where my eye rested upon a short line of carriages all bent in the direction of our home. First came father and mother, grandfather and the three younger children ; then a vehicle well known to me as that of Elias Chase from Derry Quarter ; and thus I counted them off, as one by one they drew up beside the horse-block.

I missed Sarah Sidney, who

generally came with Theophilus Baldwin's family, and having seen her placid face in its usual place on the seat beneath the gallery, fronting the meeting, I was at a loss to explain her absence. She was tenderly attached to mother, and I could not believe any light matter would take her to another's table.

A gentle voice called me to my duties :

"Why, Katherine dear, thee must have been very spry to get home before us. I was pleased to see thy interest in the meeting to-day."

The good woman kissed me and thanked me for the little aid I was able to give in unpinning her great shawl.

Directly afterward, sweet Jane Spencer came tripping up the stairs. She was frequently spoken of as exhibiting "overmuch ardor" in all her good works, but we children loved the enthusiastic little woman.

"O Katherine, I am glad to make use of thy quick fingers. My cap strings are sadly awry. I have been most uncomfortable in them all through meeting. Our breakfast was a trifle late this morning, and we had far to drive."

One and another arrived, each with a thought of me. "How thee grows, child," or "Thy mother is blessed in her little helpers."

The room was well-nigh full, when someone asked the question that had been trembling on my lips.

"Where is Sarah Sidney?"

No one directly replied, but after a moment's reflection nearly all had a suggestion or a little interest in her to express.

" Methought her face bore traces of anxiety this morning. I trust she has met with no further financial disaster. Thee knows, Rhoda, she is benevolent to a surprising degree in one whose purse is not lengthy, and it is therefore a serious matter to be forced to curtail in her giving."

" Sarah is too true a follower of the Great Teacher to be long afflicted by the things of this world," replied an aged friend.

" Ah, Hannah dear," answered the first speaker, "thee has never had the bread and butter trouble, and therefore thee can hardly compass its misery."

I think we all felt the force of this argument, for Hannah was richly dowered. Presently Jane Spencer sighed :

"I cannot help wishing that Uncle Joseph would recognize

that the hand of the Lord is pointing him to Sarah Sidney."

"If such be the will of our Heavenly Father, I doubt not it will be revealed in due time," and Hannah spoke with great deliberation.

"That is quite true, and undoubtedly it is only those among us who are a trifle worldly minded, that show a disposition to hasten these things." Jane Spencer was always very meek under reproof, and I felt glad that others sustained her desire that Uncle Joseph should be a little less deliberate in his action.

"I can hardly think that he realizes Sarah's worth," said a late comer.

"On the contrary," it was Rhoda Longstreet's voice, "I am sometimes inclined to believe that his doubt rests upon his own merit. If he were one of the world's people I should say he was bashful. As it is, I shall call him slow in perceiving his adaptation to any peculiar calling."

" Thee may be right," responded Jane Spencer, and I was struck with the note of merrymaking that accompanied her words. "If so, I can only wish that somebody would give him a hint, for I really believe that Sarah has perceived their true relationship, and that her spirit is troubled with doubt since no sign is given unto her."

"Ah," interrupted Hannah, " shall we never learn that God does not wish us to call upon him for *signs?* "

Now it had chanced, although none of those present were at that time conscious of it, that Sarah Sidney had given up her seat in a friend's carriage to a person who was suffering from a weak limb, and had walked briskly along the frozen road toward our house.

Uncle Joseph, too, had chosen to leave his vehicle at home, and seeing in the distance a familiar plump little figure, he made haste to overtake her.

For a few moments they talked together of the lesser things of life. Then they fell into silence, which was at last broken by Uncle Joseph's voice.

" My mind has dwelt much to-day upon the Bible teaching of the relation of Ruth and Boaz."

I am sure the throbbing heart beneath the clear muslin kerchief of Sarah Sidney must have bounded a little at this. He went on : " Has thee ever thought it over, and applied the test to our own lives ? "

It certainly was not strange

that the good woman hesitated before she answered :

"If thee means to ask whether it has been shown to me that I am chosen of the Lord to be thy companion, I will admit that it has; but, Joseph, thee is not an old man, nor am I a young hand-maiden."

Uncle Joseph stopped short in his walk, and catching a frightened look upon the honest face beside him, he gravely said :

"It was not upon *that* relation my mind ran. I thought rather of the increased duty in this day and generation which must belong to the husbandman and his gleaners ; or in other words the responsibility of him upon whom the benefits of this world have been showered, and the loud call that is ever sounding in my ear to extend help to those who need; and it has been whispered to me that thy material goods have been slipping from thee, and—and, I wished to offer my aid."

Could one marvel if a feeling of faintness crept over the gentle Sarah, or that a beseeching look set the seal upon the awful stillness that followed? Her face grew first scarlet, then very, very white. Uncle Joseph's voice sounded strange in her ear. She feared she should fall, but as the tones grew clearer, something else impressed her.

"Sarah, thee has a more receptive spirit than my own. I have sometimes longed to see aright in regard to the formation of a closer bond with thee, and I rejoice that through my own ill-chosen speech thee has been led to point the way."

He took her trembling hand

between his own, and smiled
down upon the sweet but tearful
face; then her lips were opened,
the pain went forever out of her
heart, and she whispered only :

" Dear Joseph."

But her trial was not quite over.
We were already summoned to
the dining room when Uncle
Joseph and Sarah Sidney entered
the door together. I glanced
about me, and was certain that I
saw more than one look of satisfaction exchanged by the company
present.

The moment of silent blessing
was past. My mother moved as
if to begin serving the soup, but
she caught Uncle Joseph's eye,
and awaited his slow words :

" Dear friends," he said with a
little tremor in his voice, " rejoice with me, for to-day has our
beloved Sarah Sidney revealed to

me the message that the Lord has given into her keeping."

He paused, and with a flush brightening her soft cheeks Sarah asked calmly :

" Joseph, will thee kindly explain thyself ? "

I never knew him to do anything so well as he now related to us the manner in which he had obtained an insight into the secret knowledge of Sarah Sidney's heart.

As he ceased speaking, her own rhythmic tones filled the room in tender thanksgiving to the Lord for his gift of companionship, and this has evermore remained in my memory as one of the most beautiful supplications I have been privileged to hear

MY GRANDAME'S SECRET.

MY GRANDAME'S SECRET.

ALMOST a hundred years ago, there was born into a staid Quaker household a child whose very physique set at defiance all the rules of the orderly family.

The father, Daniel, and the mother, Lucretia Chester, were fair, colorless persons, and the brown hair of· the latter was severely banded beneath her clear muslin cap. One can imagine the tinge of dismay that must have clouded the fatherly affection for his firstborn, when Daniel perceived that the babe was a dimpled, dark-eyed daughter, whose wealth of raven locks fell into soft rings about her brow.

As she grew into recognition of her immediate surroundings, her abounding vivacity made her singularly attractive. Her great eyes sparkled as she cooed in sympathy with the soft-toned stroke of the tall clock that had rung out the hour of her mother's birth, and the play of the firelight on the pale wall inspired her to feverish exhibitions of delight. At such times Daniel laid his hand tenderly on the refractory curls, and vainly smoothing-away their pretty curves, he said, " Alas, Lucretia, a very worldling has been given to our charge. It behooves thee and me to keep an untiring watch over the little one." " She is the Lord's own, is she not ? " was the gentle reply. But to guide and to guard her after the fashion of the

stern orthodox rule was the unre-
lenting training that the father
practiced. More than once as the
years went on, he took the scissors
from the hand of his wife, with a
strange misgiving lest she har-
bored a secret pleasure in the
child's ringlets, and severely he
cut away so much of the crowning
glory as scissors could cut, only
to find an immediate renewal of
nature's willfulness, and it was
with something like reproach that
he spoke of her brilliant color.

"I wish, Dorcas, thee had more
of the mother's tint about thee,"
he said, emphasizing the plain
Quaker name they had given the
girl, as if to counteract the impression of her brilliant beauty
which increased with time.

One day as she sat at dinner,
flushed by a wild scamper across
the lawn with her playfellow, a

soft-eyed collie, straight before her hung a looking-glass which served her father in his frequent shaving trials, and the child, catching the reflection of her bright face, cried out:

" I do not see, dear father, why thee should wish me to be pale like mother. Mine is far the prettier color. She is a snowdrop, but I am the rose."

The pain Daniel felt darkened his brow. "Dorcas," he said, "thee speaks as the daughter of sin ; thy words reveal the wiles of the devil."

The sensitive girl trembled, then her brave spirit rose and despite her tears she had answer :

" Did not our Heavenly Father make us *all*, and why may I not admire myself, if I am his handi-work, as much as thee admires dear mother ? "

Her innocence touched Lucretia, who made haste to forestall a severe reproof from her husband :

" The love of the flesh is unholy, my daughter. We are bidden to strive with all the might which the Lord vouchsafes against the things of this world. To purify the heart through the working of the Holy Spirit, this is the highest good."

" I think I do not understand thee, mother. Is the rose blushing for its sin in not being made like snowdrops ? "

" Dorcas, restrain thy tongue ; and, Lucretia, perhaps we are in error not to take the child more persistently to meeting. That she is restless and disturbing to the meditations of others must not be allowed to have too much weight."

From that time forward the

active girl placed herself under
bonds to subdue her natural in-
clinations, and many a bright
spring morning she sighed as she
watched the lambs frisking in the
fields, and noted the disappoint-
ment of the collie as she refused
his invitation to a race, and with
dripping hands she smoothed and
resmoothed her curls, preparatory
to the ride to meeting. It was
hard work, too, for her to keep
awake during the long silence or
the droning tones of the preacher,
that seemed arranged in order to
lull the restless children to sleep,
but she formulated a private code
of morals, under which this trial
figured as a dispensation to school
the spirit in its early encounters
with the tempter.

Occasionally the sermon interested her. Far more frequent
was her retirement within herself,

and in misery of spirit she re-
counted the long list of her sins,
sincerely soliciting aid from on
high that they might be over-
come. Among the chief of her
trials was to make the honest con-
fession that she was not averse to
looking at her own image, and
from this constant sense of the
enormity of the transgression grew
an absolute intolerance of her
beauty. She would have become
morbid over it, but for the thoroughly healthful nature which
reveled in outdoor exercise, and
was of no mean assistance to the
busy father in his lesser tasks.
Dorcas was unselfish, too, and her
mind turned readily into other
channels than that of self-con-
sciousness. She was a deft little
housemaid, and imitated her
mother's kindly ways with the servants ; but perhaps the absence

of childish companions gave her
an air of maturity hardly in accord
with her years. She was dreamy
too. Somewhere in her nature
lurked a drop of Southern blood ;
that which colored her rich dark
skin colored also her mental constitution. She was filled with
romance and yet she had never
heard a fairy-tale or listened to a
troubadour's song, but her soul
was on fire at the relation of a
heroic deed, or the unspoken sentiment of a pair of lovers.

Lucretia had chosen to teach
the little maiden at home; perhaps
the staid father had hesitated to
send the worldling into the midst
of temptations such as lurk behind
the schoolroom door. His pride .
in her ready insight must have
been great for he did not scorn
knowledge, although he scorned
honors, and Dorcas displayed a

marvelous aptitude for study.
Even this bore a cross to him.
" She is more like a boy than a
girl at books," he thought, and
cherished the memory of every
gentle womanly exhibition.

Daniel dearly loved Lucretia.
She was to him a type of the true
wife, and undemonstrative as he
was, little as she would have acknowledged the wish, there lurked
in the heart of each an unspeakable
sorrow that the only child which
God had given to their arms should
be so unlike the meek and patient
woman, the sweet orthodox saint,
who had borne her.

In 1815 prison reform was a
dim dream in the hearts of a few.
Men incline toward a theory of
retributive justice, and are keen
to assume the judgment rôle and
fasten a stigma to sin, forgetful
that although the sin may be out-

grown, the stigma rarely is wiped away.

The orthodoxy of society was as fixed as the theological dogma of that early day ; leniency was license to the common mind ; and the culprit was faced with continual reminders of his guilt as a necessary step toward repentance.

The wrath of man, like the wrath of God, was to be known and feared ; the evil-doer was beaten into the path of the righteous, not led by the law of love. Too much of this spirit exists at the present time, but seventy-five years ago the force of public opinion tended in that direction.

The prisoners were permitted to come forth on Sabbath morning and listen, many of them with bound limbs, to a long exhortation from the strait-laced clergy, who pointed a finger of scorn as well as reproach at the guilty, and it was little wonder that their hearts were hardened by what they heard, and that when they went forth again into the world it was often with a determination to revenge themselves on society at large.

The home of Daniel and Lucretia Chester was a resting place for such Friends as repaired to that locality for religious purposes, and Daniel was frequently charged with bearing one of them company to the county jail, which stood on the outskirts of their little town. Here he never failed to be impressed with the terrors of sin, and to exhort his family afterward to tread the straight and narrow way. More than once Dorcas had been allowed to accompany her father on such visits, with the idea of permeating the maiden's consciousness with a correct view of righteous punishment. On such an occasion, when she had just passed her sixteenth birthday, the Friend who had a " concern " to speak to the erring, aroused her indignation by his harsh denunciations. So touched was she that her sympathies far outran her judgment, and in passing through the room where the prisoners had assembled for worship, Dorcas let her eyes rove over the throng and tender smiles play about her mouth. One face among the many never faded from her memory. He was but a lad, scarcely greater in years than herself, but tall and well built. His keen glance was riveted to her face from the instant of her entrance, and when she kindly nodded to the sullen group, this youth fairly started from his seat.

His bronze brow, his piercing black eyes, his clean-cut limbs— all were instantly photographed upon her mind.

She lingered a moment at the door, while Daniel turned his carryall, and as she paused, she was conscious that the boy had reached far over his companions and was eagerly watching her.

" Father," she said, " does thee suppose all those prisoners are really guilty ? "

" Undoubtedly, Dorcas. It is a sad sight—a sad sight; but there is no room to doubt that punish- ment awaits them hereafter as well as here."

" I do not believe it," she said sternly; " that is, dear father, I do not think our Heavenly Parent will afflict them always, because they have done wrong once. Would not thee take one of them to thy home and heart after his release just as eagerly as thee would have done before he was put in prison ? "

" No, I would not. Are we not told that the way of the trans-gressor is hard, and are we to set our judgment in defiance of that of the Lord our God ? It is our duty to enforce punishment for sin, to make the sinner feel his peril, his exclusion, in order that he may repent."

" But suppose he has repented ? "

" Then let him come before his Maker and confess."

" I think it would be awfully hard, dear father, for me to go before thee and mother and say I was sorry, after you had so severely shown your displeasure with me. Now if we held out our hands and welcomed the sinner home, would he not be more likely to come?

Was it not so in the parable of the Prodigal Son ? "

"There be those," Daniel answered, as if in protest, "who thus construe the passage, but I believe it not. No man may even turn to his father's house until he has been fed on husks."

The midsummer heat was upon the land. The red sun set in splendor, and the blood-dyed moon rose as in wrath.

The simple little chamber which was Dorcas' own, had a broad window opening upon the upper veranda. The small white cot was close at its side, and the sweet night wind that bore the breath of the wild rose and the clustering honeysuckle, softly stirred the dark curls that strayed beneath the border of the muslin cap which the sleeper wore. The heat was so great that she had suffered the strings to remain untied, and the collar of her plain gown was turned away from the white throat. She stirred. Was the breath from the garden too free upon her cheek? Consciousness of some invasion made her restless. Presently her eyelids quivered and lifted; surely Dorcas was dreaming! and yet, no; there was a manly figure resting on the sill of the open window. She sat up, making a quick motion to close the neck of her gown, and tie the cap strings, but as quickly a voice broke upon her ear.

"Do not be afraid. I have been here several minutes wanting to tear off one of those strings, but I knew it would disturb you."

Dorcas was never a coward, and her astonishment at this matter-of-fact statement forbade any outcry.

"Who is thee, and what does thee want?" was her commonplace exclamation.

"I am Henri Beauclaire. I have escaped from the jail. You saw me there. I found out who you were after I was certain that it was not an angel who smiled on me last Sunday, and—do not stop me. I only want to tell you this : when I made up my mind to get out of that mad house, I made up my mind, too, that I would see you and talk to you before I went away."

The girl was fascinated by the picture. A handsome youth with his soul blazing in his eyes, sitting upright in the brilliant moonlight that fell across her bed. There was no evil in his face. She kept silent and let him speak on.

"Your name is Dorcas Chester,

and I want you to know that I
never stole the money I was put
in jail for stealing ; but they
proved I did, and so I had two
whole years to serve if I did not
get away from them. Would not
you have tried to get out ? That
is hell over there."

" Yes," she half whispered.

" I knew you would. Nothing I
can ever do or say will make me
anything in this world but a jail-
bird unless I hide. So I am going
to France for a while. My *grandpère* is there. By and by I will
come back, and you must give me
something that I can show you
then so that you will know me, for
I shall not look like this."

He glanced disdainfully at the
poor clothes he wore, and reached
out a hand as if to receive an
offering.

" What shall I give thee ? I

have nothing." A thought of a lock of her hair was in Dorcas' mind, but she knew it would be missed, cut as cleverly as she might. Then came the doubt, too, whether it were right to thus encourage a culprit !

" Give me," Henri said, and his voice was melodious, "give me that cap string."

She shrank back into the shadow. It seemed indelicate to let him touch her nightgarb.

" Would it, would it make thee think of leading a better life, of God and forgiveness and——"

" It would make me think of you, and that is of God. Forgiveness I need not, for I never did the deed. No better life ask I than such one as my *grandpère* lives."

He reached for the cap string.

Mechanically Dorcas tore it off and lifted it to his height.

The boy looked out at the sweet stars paling under the tropical moon, then he bent his eyes upon the beautiful girl, and slowly said :

"I am going now. Remember, I never did it, and keep yourself just as you are until that day when the white cap string shall come home again." He was gone, and Dorcas sat silent for a moment; then the painful consciousness forced itself upon her that her father's voice was calling. She dropped her head upon the pillow, wrapped the sheet about her throat, and closed her eyes. The voice came nearer. "Dorcas, Dorcas," it said ; but she did not stir. Her heart was wildly beating with fear lest the youth of her dream should be pursued, but her parent went calmly away, and only at breakfast was there any allusion to the circumstance.

" Dorcas, thee talked strangely, last night, in thy sleep."

The girl's face crimsoned as she felt the untruthfulness of her reply : " How funny that is ! " but the motherly eye was not long without discovering the loss of the nightcap string.

" Daughter," she said, " how was it possible for thee to tear thy cap in this way ? It is as though thee had willed to do it and done it with all thy might."

And the girl replied, with some of her hoydenish spirit : " Throw the old thing away ; I have plenty more," for it seemed as if she could not tolerate the witness to her secret compact.

" I am surprised," answered the gentle mother. " Waste not, want not. Get thy thimble and thread ; here is some muslin, thee can hem another string."

Dorcas did not allow herself to brood over her midnight adventure. Perhaps she was pained by the part of concealment that she played toward her parents; perhaps she was troubled, too, by a recollection of the rebuke contained in the boy's words. She was sometimes inclined to feel that he was right and her own little world was wrong in so strictly upholding law, and in believing the ways of God were at utter variance from the ways of generous men.

"I care not to live any better life than that *mon grandpère* lives."

These words were ringing in her ears, and she pictured to herself the detail of that life, far enough from reality, no doubt, but a pretty idyl. She began to read much history, and once asked her mother to allow her to take French

lessons from a villager. Lucretia was shocked.

"Ah, my child ! there is little to
be read in that tongue that could
benefit thee. Blasphemers and
winebibbers they are, with no
sense of shame in their idolatry of
sensual things."

" Then they are an evil-minded
people, mother ? "

" Yea, yea; a frivolous and false-
hearted race."

Then Dorcas turned away
sorrowfully. Could it be that
Henri Beauclaire had told what
was not true ? If he could steal
he might also lie. He was base
had he done both; and if that race
was false why was he an exception among Frenchmen ? When
this mood was upon her she
blushed alone in her chamber at
the thought of the bit of muslin
that he so carefully rolled about

his finger and put from sight.
Mostly, however, her meditations
were concluded with the memory
of his respect for the clean life of
his *grandpère*, and, do as she
might, to think him guilty she
could not.

The years went quickly by. It
was a round of simple duties to
Dorcas, enlivened by a keen sense
of the beautiful and a quick response to sympathetic needs.
The weeks were much alike.
First-day meeting, followed by the
household laundry work. Fourth-
day meeting, succeeded by the
mending, sweeping, and baking.
This was varied by monthly meeting day dinner, when several
Friends were apt to be seated at
their board, or a drive to a
quarterly meeting in a larger
community; and the crowning
event—not often enjoyed by Lu-

cretia and Dorcas—of passing a week in the great city at the time of the yearly gathering. It was on one of the latter occasions that Dorcas met and became much interested in a young man who was welcomed by Daniel as the son of a dear and distant friend. She had never mingled with youth a great deal, and George Townsend's quick wit and good temper were a source of great pleasure to her. She had no idea of marriage in her mind, and when, after months of intimate acquaintance, he directly asked her to become his wife, she shrank from him as if he had struck her.

"Does thee feel that I have done wrong?" he gently questioned.

"No," she stammered; but a strange vision of flashing dark eyes and an earnest injunction to

" keep just as you are now " made her faint.

" Will thee let me dwell upon thy request in solitude ? " she said, and the honest-hearted man made answer :

" Thee is right to question thy own soul. If there thee finds a single cloud, wait until the light cometh."

When Dorcas sat alone she covered her face with both hands and a few tears trickled between her fingers. Presently she wiped them away, and began to question herself as she would have questioned another.

" Why do I hesitate? I am greatly drawn toward George Townsend. Father and mother regard him highly ; he is a God-fearing man, capable and conscientious ; he is a member of our meeting ; his business can be readily arranged so that we may live near my dear parents and bless their declining years. Why not ?"

To so pure a maiden, one whose affections had never keenly asserted themselves nor been lightly trifled with, the idea of having granted unasked the treasure of her love was in itself a reproach.

Dorcas paled in view of the thought to which she felt it right to give definite shape ; then she walked restlessly toward the window where once sat the dark-eyed lad, and she said, honestly and bravely :

"Until to-day the actual meaning of that charge, to 'keep as you are,' never occurred to me. Am I certain that he intended that bit of muslin to typify my faith—faith to him personally ? or was it, as I vaguely comprehended it then, faith that I would be the same in my just dealing with his apparent shortcomings? Who can tell? It is six years since he went away. Perhaps he died before seeing his *grandpère* again. Perhaps he forgot the place where he suffered so much; or found his beautiful ancestral home too lovely to leave. Perhaps—" and this hurt her, but she thought it fair to admit the doubt, " perhaps he fell into evil ways again. And, indeed, had he been all that my dream pictured, would he not, within six years, have found an opportunity to communicate with me? Surely I deserved it."

Then came another question; " Would I have married him, had he come back with a clean record and a demand for my love? Could I have given my life into the hand of an utter stranger, a foreigner of whose race I know no good? Would my father and mother have blessed me and bade me go to my husband's arms with joy? No, it could not have been, and I could not have done it without. Should Henri return to-morrow for the fulfillment of such a desire, I should bid him leave me. Is it right to marry George Townsend with this secret in my heart? Ought I to reveal it, reveal my doubts and struggles concerning it? No. I should be quite willing to place my hand in his and say, 'George, whatever thee has in thy heart that thee wishes to tell me, that do I wish to hear; but whatever trials thee has passed through and honestly left behind thee, with those I have no question.'

"Could I let George go from me and live my life alone, without a pang because of his absence? No, I could not. Therefore, O Lord, with a clean heart I will walk beside him, asking daily grace from thy hand, and humbly seeking to serve thee through serving him."

She bathed her flushed face, smoothed the curls away, and went into the garden. There among the sweet-peas and the rich clove-pinks, she laid her hand in that of her lover and simply said :

"My heart tells me I will be a true wife unto thee."

The next decade wrought a great change in Dorcas. The vivacity that she had seemed so likely to lose under the stern repression of her parents, assumed the semblance of loving good cheer. Her beauty as a matron surpassed that of her girlhood, and it became a matter of merry-making in the household that a stranger never passed her without turning to look a second time. Her sweet spirit was overflowing with thankfulness for the great blessing of fervid affection from so manly and upright a companion as George Townsend. Indeed, if ever the taint of pride clung to Dorcas it was when she thought of her husband.

A little maiden had for eight years walked beside her. A faithful representative of the Chester household. Truly, if Daniel had regretted his own daughter's alien features, he was content now in the miniature Lucretia whose demure air was a marked contrast to the flashing wit of her dark-eyed mother.

The village, too, was changed. Through George Townsend's exertions manufacturing interests flourished, and although wealth was pouring into his coffers, the comfort of a thousand lesser households told of just dealing between man and man. But the old jail still stood on the highway, and its barred windows were lengthened to a half score. The same fiery brick walls, the same foul atmosphere, the same class of inhabitants were closed behind the multitudinous bolts and bars. The passer-by winced as he heard the loud laugh or the fearful curse; and the faces that pressed against the iron casement were faces of the young and the old, of women as well as men, and gathered from the ranks of first offenders as well as those of the hardened criminals.

One morning, while yet Dorcas sat at the head of the breakfast table, dispensing as much of cheer by her sunny face as from the viands, a message was brought requesting her presence at the county jail. It was no unusual occurrence for the mother to be thus summoned from her peaceful home to smooth the path of the unrighteous, and very shortly she stepped from her carriage into the door of the plague spot of the neat village. She was met by the jailer's wife, a coarse woman, but not untouched with good intentions.

"I was sorry to send for you," she said, "but a queer-looking man was let in last night, who has been bleeding at the lungs, and all I could do and say was nothing till I promised to fetch you early this morning. He hadn't ought to been here, I 'spose, but Thomas found him sitting on the door-step, and rattling the latch, and

when he asked to be let in and
Thomas said as it was a jail, he up
and told a queer story about once
having broke out; and anyways
it wasn't right to leave him out
there a-bleedin', so I put him in
one of my rooms; he seemed de-
cent-like."

An unaccustomed horror crept
over Dorcas. She had to steady
herself against the door-post for
a moment before following the
woman into the cramped little
chamber.

Half-sitting upon the bed, surrounded with pillows and cloths
stained with blood, was Henri
Beauclaire. His eyes flashed with
the old intensity, but from amid
the pallor of a countenance wasted
with disease.

"Stand there," he whispered
hoarsely; and motioning to the
jailer's wife to go out, he fastened

his gaze on Dorcas' half-fright-
ened face.

"Look at me, woman ; do you
know me?"

She bowed her head.

"Do you know what this is?"
he said again, as he drew from
his breast a bit of soiled and
yellow muslin.

"This is a betrothal ring. Yes,
I tell you, by this you plighted
your troth to me, and by the
heavens above, you have broken
your faith."

Dorcas made motion as if to
answer.

"Stop," he said. "You can
have nothing to say ; it is I who
must relieve my bursting heart.
Do you know what this is?" laying his finger on the bright stains.
"This is my life-blood, and you
have spilled it. When I came
over sea I had a cough, and they

told me I needed care, but I laughed them to scorn, for I said to myself, when once I am there, where her gentle hands can smooth the pain away and her sweet smile bring back the light to my eyes, all will be well. Do you know how it was with me during these years ? When, after being hunted like a wild beast from wood to cavern, from hill to seaport, at last I stood by my *grandpère,* his heart was filled with joy—for I was his only descendant left on earth, and on me he leaned feeble and childish. I could not leave him for an hour without reproach ; how could I come to you ? Year after year he lingered, and although I starved for your smile, I believed in you, and God knows, had I suspected the awful truth of your unfaithfulness, I should have done the same. Heaven itself could

not have lured me from that poor
man, whose dying blessing is
sounding in my ears this day.
When I had laid him away, scarce
three months ago, and found that
the old chateau with its thousands
of meters of rich garden and til-
lage was mine, I bounded for
my passport, I dreamed of naught
else than a return to build a family worthy of the saintly dead.

"Would you know the rest?
How I came in the dusk to the
village street and crept in the
shadow to your father's door, feeling that I could not at once bear
the blaze of your beauty. When I
had seen the old man open the
casement and sit in the moonlight
with a child upon his knee, my
heart misgave me. Fainting for
food, for I had been too eager to
eat, I crept back to the inn. Slowly
I questioned the *garçon* concern-

ing the people of the village, and
gradually the truth dawned—you
were untrue! I was like a mad-
man that night. I wore a track
in the floor, I doubt not, with my
restless pacing, and when day
broke I went forth with a wild
intent to do murderous work.
All through the hours of sunlight
I examined the mill, and the
dwelling-place where a false heart
was beating, and at night I planned
to carry out my work of destruc-
tion. I would fire the mill and
the house and take care that, so
quick would leap the flames, that
no escape would be possible. And
if, through some strange fatality,
my plot was defeated, there, in the
fierce distraction of a great con-
flagration, I would rush upon you
with my knife and stab you to
your death! Yes," he leaned
forward and hissed the words,

"the woman who has taught me
that there is no faith, that God
and honor and love are myths,
ought to die by the hand of the
man whom she has wrecked."

Again Dorcas stirred, and again
he waved her into silence.

"And what was your excuse?
Six years of silence. What were
they to me? Six centuries might
have waned, and I should have
kept my faith. When I looked at
this trysting string, I said alway
and ever the same: 'She is as
strong as the threads she tore
with so great an effort; she will
never waver.'

"What was the good of nature's
brand that you bear: the mark of
unyielding purpose, of faith and
love as firm as God's foundation,
as broad as the firmament—you
belie them all. There you stand
now with your great eyes shining

as if a *soul* dwelt behind them; your rich smooth skin blooming with the color and purity of nature, not artifice ; your red lips curved with a smile you cannot repress, and yet I swear you are as false as hell !

" Only this "— he touched the crimson stains—" only this defeated my plan, and enabled you to breath the sweet spring air once more; only this has made it possible for me to die cursing you with my latest breath without dealing that blow at your heart that should have mingled our blood in one stream."

The exhausted man fell back upon his pillows, and Dorcas crept to his side and smoothed the rich waves of jet-black hair, and with a wet sponge moistened his lips. Presently he opened his eyes, and before he could speak she said calmly :

"I am going to take thee to our home. George Townsend will help me to nurse thee back to life and peace. I will tell thee, now, that I never knew thy full intent in asking me for the cap string; had I known it I should not have given it, for thy reason and my own would have rebelled against an alliance wholly at variance with Nature's laws. Thee did not love *me*, the girl; thee loved my *faith*, my trust in thy honesty; and I bid thee go on loving it, for I shall trust thee now, just as I trusted thee then. I believed thee inno-cent of the crime for which thee had been confined. I believed it only because thee said it was so, and thy face told the same story. I believe in thee now, in despite thy *words*, for thy soul is speaking more truly through thy glance, and that tells me that thy devotion to thy *grandpère* was no myth, while thy frenzy is. Thee shall find thy faith in me is rewarded, for thee shall live to be one of our household and to bless us all with thy goodness."

She ceased speaking, summoned the jailer's wife, and had the sick man borne to her carriage.

When she had reached her own door Dorcas entered alone, and quietly spoke to her husband, who still sat by the breakfast table.

" George, I have brought home a very ill man ; will thee please attend to his removal from the carriage while I prepare a bed ? I shall put him into the little room next our own that I may the more carefully tend him."

That night, as Dorcas sat late by the invalid's side, the only word that he spoke was the whispered question :

" Are you not afraid ? "

And as she bent over him tenderly she answered :

" Not for a moment do I fear thee ; I only wish thee well."

Slowly the strength came to the feeble pulse, but when the frail man was permitted to leave his sick bed, it was found that his cough became less frequent and his fever had subsided. Then, too, he was moved into a large upper chamber, the best the house afforded, and although the kind attentions of Dorcas were unremitted, he lost all sense of care or espionage. Gradually he recognized himself as a member of the family, and never was there any allusion to his advent or expected departure. Before many months he was the dear "uncle," of the household, taking his part in all that went on ; teaching the little

Lucretia ; reading aloud bits of quaint wisdom or humor, from " Le Roman de la Rose," and " Le Roman du Renart ; " pages from Froissart, his beloved Pascal, and La Bruyère ; or listening to the many schemes for lifting the burdens of others that were constantly suggested by George or Dorcas.

From 1820 to 1830 there was a great awakening on the subject of Prison Reform. The work of England's noble Howard had been supplemented by that of the devoted Elizabeth Fry, and the whole world rang with their achievements. Slow, alas ! was the motion across the water, but sure in its coming.

Henri Beauclaire, too feeble to exert great physical effort, was keenly alive to the necessity of introducing humanitarian methods in all places for the confinement of the accused.

He labored unceasingly toward an enlargement and purification of the county jail, for separate day rooms for the men and women, for decent food and lavatories, and for constant occupation. In all he did Henri was warmly seconded by his true friends, and when at last the summons came that called him from their midst, no one among the villagers was more regretted.

In the short will which was found amid his small effects, he had bequeathed the old chateau to his native town as a home for such discharged prisoners as were friendless and aged, and the closing clause read thus :

"'To my more than sister, my earthly savior, Dorcas Townsend, I leave the testimony of my later years, and the contents of my strong-box."

This contained some valuable silver and household linen bear-ing a coronet, and a sandalwood casket wherein reposed a yellow muslin cap string.

In the evening following the burial Dorcas sat with her family about her on the moonlit porch. She slid her hand softly into that of her husband, and said :

" George dear, thee has never asked me, but I should like to tell thee, the secret of my peculiar interest in our brother who has passed away."

Then my grandame told the story, and the accurate memory of my mother gave it unto me as it is written.

At its conclusion her husband kissed her flushed cheek, saying :

" Thine was ever a romantic

nature, and were romance always controlled by reason, how many lives might blossom into joy and usefulness, as did that of our beloved Henri."

THE END.